# The Contrast

## A Comedy in Five Acts

### By

### Royall Tyler

Published by Forgotten Books 2012

Originally Published 1920

PIBN 1000195605

# THE CONTRAST

# THE
# CONTRAST

A COMEDY

*In Five Acts* ↩

*By* ROYALL TYLER

---

With a *History of George Washington's Copy* by
JAMES BENJAMIN WILBUR

---

BOSTON & NEW YORK
HOUGHTON MIFFLIN COMPANY
MDCCCCXX

Copy 2

*15.00*

# PREFACE

IN reproducing in a separate volume a play of the eighteenth, in this the twentieth century, the writer feels certain of interesting all students of early American drama and literature, and especially so, since it has been possible to present for the first time, in the Introduction by the granddaughter of Royall Tyler, new and interesting information about the author, the play, and the times in which it was written.

Montrose J. Moses, in his "Representative Plays," says: "Whether the intrinsic merits of the play would contribute to the amusement of audiences to-day is to be doubted, although it is a striking dramatic curio. The play in the reading is scarcely exciting. It is surprisingly devoid of situation. Its chief characteristic is 'talk,' but that talk, reflective in its spirit of 'The School for Scandal,' is interesting to the social student."

In those days the reading of the play, if we can judge by the newspapers of the time, proved highly interesting to a large audience in Philadelphia, where Wignell was unable to give the play on the stage owing to a disagreement with

the principal actors, though we can hardly imagine many to-day paying for the privilege of
hearing a play read, especially one with very little plot, and little if any dramatic denouement.

As "The School for Scandal" was in some
sense a product of its time, so "The Contrast," if
read discerningly, throws a very interesting side
light on the taste and manners of American society in 1787, long before modern plays with their
quick action and dialogue and their artistic scen-
ery, to say nothing of the breath-taking real-
ism of the moving-pictures, had worked their
changes in the American theatre. There is no
doubt it was a successful play at the time. It is
difficult to visualize New York with a popula-
tion of about thirty thousand people, yet it was
then, as it ever has been, the first city of the North
American continent, and to fill its principal
theatre with the best people of the city more
than once was a strong endorsement for any production.

It is said that men of action have always been
fond of the theatre; we know that Washington
was, as was Lincoln. And now we approach the
second reason for the present reprint of Royall
Tyler's play "The Contrast." George Washington, the President of the United States, was

[*Facsimile, slightly reduced*]

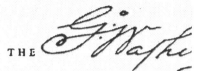

THE

# CONTRAST,

A

# COMEDY;

IN FIVE ACTS:

WRITTEN BY A

CITIZEN OF THE *UNITED STATES;*

Performed with Applause at the Theatres in NEW-YORK,
PHILADELPHIA, and MARYLAND;

AND PUBLISHED *(under an Assignment of the Copy-Right)* BY

# THOMAS WIGNELL.

---

Primus ego in patriam
Aonio——deduxi vertice Musas.
         VIRGIL.
*( Imitated.)*

First on our shores I try THALIA's powers,
And bid the *laughing, useful* Maid be ours.

---

## PHILADELPHIA:

FROM THE PRESS OF *PRICHARD & HALL*, IN MARKET STREET;
BETWEEN SECOND AND FRONT STREETS.

M. DCC. XC.

among the first subscribers for the published play, of which he received two copies. He wrote his name in one and placed it in his library.[1]

Pursuing the further fortunes of this copy of "The Contrast," I begin by quoting from L. E. Chittenden's "Personal Reminiscences, 1840–1890."

"Many years ago," says Mr. Chittenden, "I began to collect books relating to Vermont printed before 1850. . . . Omitting the pursuit of the numerous pamphlets touching the controversy between New York and Vermont, relating to the New Hampshire grants, which are now worth more than their weight in silver, as shown by the prices paid for them at the Brinley sale, I will come at once to a legend which has ripened into a fact, in the history of the American theatre. The legend was that the first play written by an American author ever represented upon the American stage was written by a Vermonter, named Royal Tyler. He was known to have been a lawyer, a justice of the Vermont Supreme Court, a celebrated wit, a well-known contributor to the 'Farmer's Museum,' published at Walpole, New Hampshire, by Isaiah Thomas. Tyler had made an acciden-

[1] See Note on page xviii.

tal visit to New York City, where he had formed
the acquaintance of Thomas Wignell, a leading
comedian, who wished to introduce to the stage
the character of Brother Jonathan. Judge Tyler
had accordingly written the comedy of 'The
Contrast,' in which Brother Jonathan was a
principal character. It had been performed with
great eclat in New York, Philadelphia, Baltimore, and Washington to crowded houses. It
was a part of the legend that the play, under the
name of 'The Contrast,' had been printed and
published in New York City about the year
1790.

"A play with such a history, written by a
Vermonter, would be a veritable nugget in the
literature of the Green Mountain State. The
title stood at the head of my list of 'wants' for
almost twice fifteen years. But the chase for it
was never hopeful. No copy of it was ever discovered, nor any evidence, except the legend
that it had been printed. If it had ever been published, it must have been in a pamphlet form.
Pamphlets are invariably short lived. The respect which insures preservation cannot be secured without covers. Put covers upon any pamphlet and it becomes a book, to be protected
against the waste basket and the rag bag; it se-

cures the respect of the house wife and the servant, those peripatetic and most dangerous ene-
mies of the treasures of the book collector.

"In the chase for 'The Contrast,' I had employed all the recognized means of getting upon
the track of a rare book. I had patiently examined all the auction and sale catalogues for years.
I had standing orders for 'The Contrast' with
all the booksellers. I had handled many, possibly hundreds of cords of the trash in Gowan's
and other second-hand dealers, and the result
had been nil. Not only had no copy of the play
been discovered, but I had not found a particle
of evidence that it had ever been printed.

"The play could scarcely be a century old.
If printed, its date could not have been earlier
than 1790. Surely a book of a date so recent
could not have wholly ceased to exist. I was fi-
nally forced to the conclusion that the legend
was erroneous, that 'The Contrast' had never
been printed.

"This decision of mine was published in some
newspapers and came to the knowledge of a lin-
eal descendant of Judge Tyler, a reputable citizen of Boston. To convince me of my error, he
sent me one printed leaf of the play, comprising
pages 45 and 46. At the top of each page was

the title 'The Contrast.' In the dialogue were the characters 'Brother Jonathan' and 'Jenny' and the former sang the song 'Yankee Doodle.' These pages settled the fact that the play had been printed. The printing was proved; the disappearance of the last printed copy I was compelled to regard as impossible to be accounted for by the rules which commonly determine the life of a book.

"The wheels of time rolled on to the year 1876. I had given up all hope of 'The Contrast'; the mystery continued unexplained and grew darker with age. One day I received a catalogue entitled 'Washingtoniana. Books, rare plans and maps, a part of the library of General George Washington. Many of the books contain his autograph. To be sold in Philadelphia on Tuesday afternoon, November 26th, 1876, by Thomas and Sons, auctioneers.' No. 35 of this catalogue contained this title, 'The Contrast, a comedy in 5 acts. Frontispiece. 8vo. Morocco. Philadelphia, 1790. Has autograph.'

"Was this the 'Contrast' which I had hunted so long, or some other? It was printed in Philadelphia, the genuine was supposed to have been printed in New York. Yet the date 1790 was about correct. But why was it in the library of

General George Washington? This was a very
suspicious circumstance, after the forgery of his
motto 'Exitus acta probat,' and his book plate,
which was imposed upon so many collectors.
But it was unsafe to attract attention to the title
by correspondence. Slight as the chance was, I
determined not to lose it. I employed a well-
known bookseller and bibliophile of New York
City to attend the sale, and if this was the genuine 'Contrast' to buy it without limit of price.
I was very confident that, after so long a chase,
the genuine comedy was worth as much to me
as to any other collector.[1] . . .

[1] "Yesterday afternoon at the Thomas auction rooms the last volumes of the Library of General George Washington were scattered to
the winds by the last heir of the family, Lawrence Washington. This
young man, who was present at the sale, is a great-grandson of General
Washington's brother and a son of the late Jno. A. Washington. Mr.
Washington is a dark-complexioned young man, of medium height
and size, who only recently came into possession of the property. Before the sale began Mr. Jennings of the firm of Thomas & Sons explained the reason for it. The books were stored in a room of a house
belonging to the family, which was rented to a Pennsylvanian, who
promised that it should be kept constantly locked. When Mr. Washington examined the library, he found that the promise had not been
kept; that volumes had disappeared, the autographs had been clipped
from others, and that there was danger that the whole collection would
be scattered in a few years. There was no doubt whatever of the
authenticity of the volumes at this time. The sale then proceeded,
there being a large number of literary men, librarians, booksellers, and
private collectors present.

"In the Washington Collection there were 138 lots and in all
about 250 volumes. The total amount realized was $1933.00, with
which price the auctioneer expressed himself entirely satisfied, saying

"My order proved a success. It secured the genuine 'Contrast,' which was purchased for a few dollars, and my agent returned with it in his possession. Its inspection showed that it formed no exception to the rule that every published book appears in commerce once in 15 years; for this play had never been published. It was printed for a list of subscribers, which appeared with the comedy. 'The President of the United States' was the first subscriber. This copy had been bound in red and green morocco, tooled and ornamented in the highest style of the bibliopegistic art of the time, for General Washington, who then filled the exalted position of Chief Magistrate of the Republic. The title page was adorned by his well-known autograph. The volume now lies before me, perfect in every particular: with a frontispiece engraved by Maverick, one of our earliest engravers on metal, from a painting by Dunlap, containing the portraits *ad vivum* of Wignell as Brother Jonathan, Mrs. Morris as Charlotte, and three of the other principal characters in the play as

it was more than he had expected to receive. Few of the books had any value except that which had been conferred upon them by their distinguished ownership. Many were public documents of which there are numerous copies in existence and none of them were rare."

From the Philadelphia "Times," November 29, 1876.

represented. It would be difficult to imagine a volume possessing more elements of attraction to a collector than the first play written by an American, which created the stage character of Brother Jonathan, was once owned by the Father of his Country, who had written his own name upon the title, and which was withal of such excessive rarity.

"One would suppose that a volume which had so long evaded the most exhaustive and comprehensive search would be properly called unique. And yet it was not. Collectors know that it is a rule to which exceptions seldom occur, that the discovery of one very rare volume is followed by the discovery of its duplicate. I was not therefore much surprised when, a few weeks after this volume came into my hands I was informed by that careful and intelligent collector of portraits of actors and other material connected with the stage, Mr. Thomas J. McKee, that he, too, had just secured a copy of "The Contrast," at the end of a search which for length and thoroughness almost rivalled my own. He had secured it by the merest accident. A catalogue to him from some small English city, Bristol, I believe, contained its title priced at a few shillings. He ordered it, and in due course of mail received a copy of this rare and long hunted play. From his copy 'The Contrast' has recently been reprinted. That copy and the one above described are the only copies so far known of the original edition."

Forty-four years after the sale just described I purchased a priced copy of the catalogue, a facsimile of the fifth page of which is here reproduced.

From Mr. Chittenden this copy of "The Contrast" passed into the hands of Mr. Samuel P. Avery, who had been on the hunt for the book for years. Unfortunately neither of the parties to the transfer left any record of how it came about. We may assume, however, that only a very liberal offer could have persuaded Mr. Chittenden to part with the cherished volume, though it is possible that it may have come to Mr. Avery indirectly.

In an endeavor to trace the history of the copy at this point, I applied to the librarian of the University of Vermont, to which Mr. Chittenden had given his collection of books and pamphlets relating to Vermont, which included many rare items, but could learn nothing from that source, the librarian having no information as to this copy of "The Contrast."

POLITICAL PAMPHLETS, containing—Dissertation *13. 00*
on the Political Union of the Thirteen United
States, Phila., 1783; Sketches of American
Policy, by Noah Webster, Hartford, 1785;
Observations on the American Revolution,
Phila., 1789; Rights of Man, by Tom Paine,
Phila., 1791, and several other pamphlets, 2
vols. 8vo, calf.

☞ Each volume has Autograph.

BORDLEY. J. B. — On Husbandry and Rural *8. 50*
Affairs, 8vo, calf.                      Phila , 1799
☞ Has Autograph.

BUFFON'S Natural History, abridged, numerous *5. 00*
illustrations, 2 vols. 8vo, calf.   London, 1792

☞ Each volume has Autograph.

BELKNAP. JEREMY—History of New-Hampshire, *11. 00*
with Map, 3 vols. 8vo, sheep.      Phila., 1784

☞ Each volume has Autograph.

Contrast. The—A Comedy in Five Acts, frontis- *2 0.00*
piece, 8vo, morocco.                Phila., 1790
☞ Has Autograph.

MOORE. JOHN—View of Society and Manners in *9 00*
Italy, 2 vols. 8vo, sheep.          London, 1783

☞ Each volume has Autograph and Coat-of-Arms.

MOORE. JOHN—View of Society and Manners in *8. 50*
France, Switzerland and Germany, 2 vols.
8vo, sheep.                         London, 1783
☞ Each volume has Autograph and Coat-of-Arms.

SWIFT. ZEPHANIAH—System of the Laws of the *11 00*
State of Connecticut, 2 vols. 8vo, sheep.
Windham, 1795      .
☞ Each volume has Autograph.

JEFFERSON. THOS.—Notes on the State of Vir- *16. 00*
ginia, second edition, 8vo, shp.   Phila., 1794
☞ Has Autograph.

It was known, however, that Mr. Avery had obtained the book, and as it was reported that he had given it to Columbia University, I who had myself long sought to add this item to my collection of Vermontiana, had almost given up hope, when — with what joy you who are collectors can imagine — I received Anderson's catalogue listing the prize. But alas! would my bank balance hold out when it was put up for sale? Just at that time a spectacular purchase in London by one of our well-known booksellers brought out the following on the editorial page of the New York *Times*:

## "THAT PRICE WAS NOT FOR A BOOK

" Lovers of books for what is in them rather than for what they are feel a sort of irritation when they read, as they did yesterday, about the payment of what, when exchange was normal, would have been $75,000 for a little volume the only merit of which is that no other copy of the same edition is known to be in existence. There are nobody knows how many thousand other editions of the same work, all of them as good or better than this one, in the eyes of the reader as distinguished from the collector, and most of them can be bought any day and anywhere for a dollar or two.

" The collector, however, has a reason for being, and he serves several innocent and even useful purposes. His only, or chief, fault is that he claims — and too often the claim is admitted — to be a lover of books and to have a relation to literature. In reality, it is not books that interest him, but irrelevant things like dates and bindings and associations with departed greatness. In other words, he is a curio hunter, and what he calls his 'library' is a museum where the reading man finds next to nothing that he wants — nothing at all that he must have."

I knew that if the same dealer started after my heart's desire it would go hard with me. I had been in contests with him before and had occasionally come out with the prize, but I hoped he would not get any unlimited orders for this item or want it for himself. I could not attend the sale, being at that time indisposed, but I was immediately made well by the receipt of a telegram announcing that the prize was won.

The priced page of the Anderson catalogue is reproduced here, that collectors may see what opportunities our older friends had in the seventies. Will our books increase in value in the same cover serving for both volumes. ''The Complete Angler'' is bound in green levant morocco, with emblematic tooling of fishes in border, and red moire silk doublures; ''Walton's Lives'' is bound in brown levant morocco, gilt border, with rosettes at corners and sides, blue gros-grain silk doublures and flys. Pickering's Diamond Edition.

*5.00* 970. WALTONIANA. Inedited Remains in Verse and Prose of Izaak Walton, Author of the Complete Angler. With notes and Preface by Richard H. Shepherd. 8vo, full green levant morocco, gilt back, gilt inside borders, gilt edges, by F. Bedford.

Scarce. London: Pickering and Co., 1878

*1.00* 971. WARREN (HON. J. LEICESTER). A Guide to the Study of Book-Plates (Ex-Libris). FIRST EDITION. *Illustrated.* 8vo, cloth. London, 1880

### WITH GEORGE WASHINGTON'S AUTOGRAPH AND BOOKPLATE

*20* 972. [WASHINGTON (GEORGE).] An History of the Earth, the Animated Nature. By Oliver Goldsmith. The Second Edition. *Illustrations.* In 8 vols. Vol. VIII. 8vo, original polished calf. In a polished calf slip-case. London: J. Nourse, 1779

FROM THE LIBRARY OF GEORGE WASHINGTON, WITH HIS AUTOGRAPH ON THE TITLE-PAGE, AND HIS BOOKPLATE ON INSIDE OF FRONT COVER. This book was inherited by Laurence Washington and was sold by him at Philadelphia, Nov. 28, 1876. The set of 8 vols. was purchased by John R. Baker, who resold it in 1891. The volumes were subsequently sold separately.

### WITH GEORGE WASHINGTON'S AUTOGRAPH

*00* 973. [WASHINGTON (GEORGE).] The Contrast, A Comedy; in Five Acts: Written by a Citizen of the United States; Performed with Applause at the Theatres in New-York, Philadelphia, and Maryland; and published by Thomas Wignell, *Frontispiece designed by Wm. Dunlap and engraved by Maverick.* 8vo, contemporary American red morocco, borders and center-piece inlaid in green morocco, with conventional floriated tooling in gilt. In a maroon levant slip-case. Philadelphia: Prichard & Hall, 1790

GEORGE WASHINGTON'S COPY, WITH HIS AUTOGRAPH ON THE TITLE-PAGE. Heading the list of Subscribers is ''The President of the United States.'' The play was written by Royal Tyler of Vermont and is said to have been the first play represented by a regular company on the American stage written by a native American. Laid in is a sheet of paper with the Washington mark, a facsimile of his bookplate and a facsimile of Wignell's letter presenting Washington with two copies of this book.

*00* 974. WASHINGTON (GEORGE). George Washington to the People of the United States announcing his intention of retiring from Public Life. *With a brilliant impression of the very rare portrait by Edwin, in* FIRST STATE. Hart 360. Small folio, full old red morocco, broad gilt border surrounding an inner panel of

ratio? It hardly seems possible, but Mr. George
D. Smith, who was the premier book-buyer of
the world, believed they would. Some of us have
felt that if he could have lived twenty years
longer he would have justified his opinion.

William Loring Andrews, in "Bibliopegy in
the United States," speaking of the fine morocco binding on "Brown's Illustrated Family
Bible," 1792, says,

"Quite as creditable to its author, and belonging to the same period as the binding above
mentioned, is the one upon Washington's own
copy of 'The Contrast' (Philadelphia, MDCCXC)
a comedy written by Royal Tyler of Vermont
for Thomas Wignell, Comedian, now in the
possession of Mr. S. P. Avery, a book made
doubly valuable by having the great chieftain's
bold, clear signature upon the title-page. It is
a royal octavo, bound in a hard, close-textured,
highly polished dark red morocco, the sides inlaid with green borders, with ornamental gilt
scroll tooling. The back of the volume is elab-
orately gilt-tooled with small stamps, one of
which is the acorn, a tool so frequently used by
the Mearnes (the distinguished English biblio-
pegist predecessors of Roger Payne), as to have
become considered as reliable an indication of

their work, as is the 'sausage' pattern which appears upon so many of the bindings attributed to them. . . .

"Positive proof that this binding was executed in this country is lacking, but appearances and the circumstantial evidence in the case, point to that conclusion."

The editor of this little volume publishes it, as William Loring Andrews did his productions, largely for the pleasure it gives him, and with some hope that others may share that pleasure.

JAMES BENJAMIN WILBUR

*November*, 1920

---

NOTE: — With his two copies of *The Contrast* Washington received the following letter: —

"Mr. Wignell, with the utmost respect and deference, has the honor of transmitting to the President of the United States two copies of The Contrast.

"Philadelphia May 22nd 1790."

I wrote to the Library of Congress to see if the other copy was there and received the following reply: —

"The Library of Congress has two copies of 'The Contrast,' but, according to reports from our Division of Manucripts and from the Superintendent of the Reading Room, neither of them was Washington's. Moreover, the Union Catalogue of books in certain large libraries in this country contains no entry of any copy apparently."

A later letter states that only one of the copies in the Library of Congress is of the original edition, the other being the Dunlap Society reprint of 1887.

FACSIMILE OF BINDING OF WASHINGTON'S COPY

*(Original 5 ⅛ by 8 ¼ inches)*

# CONTENTS

# ILLUSTRATIONS

# INTRODUCTION

HE *Drama sought for a place in America from early Colonial days. Fostered in some sections, frowned upon in others, housed appropriately in some cities, elsewhere denied foothold or rooftree, the year* 1787 *found the American public divided for and against it, with theatres established in a few of the principal cities. Farces, satires, tragedies, written and printed but not acted, and the same acted but not printed, had sprung up in increasing numbers. Even in New England, where prejudice was deep-rooted against all forms of "play-acting" collegians had written, spoken, and acted dramatic pieces at College Exhibitions.*

*During the British occupancy of Boston, New York, and Philadelphia, plays were often given by them, a few of which were composed by officers. Playbills of these performances were sent to General Washington and members of his armies. Plays by writers of American birth had been published and acted in London before the Revolution.*

*The honor of having written the first tragedy to be performed on an American stage by professionals, belongs to Thomas Godfrey of Philadelphia. His* The Prince of Parthia *was played, once, in Philadelphia, April,* 1767, *at the New Southwark Theatre by the American Company. The theme of the tragedy had nothing to do with America.*

*A comic opera, dealing with local life and incidents, entitled* Disappointment, or the Force of Credulity, *written by Andrew Barton — supposed pseudonym of Colonel Forrest, of Germantown — was rehearsed by the American Company, but never performed. This play was published twice, in* 1767 *and* 1797. *Before* 1787 *there had been no play written epitomizing the opposing characteristics of the young United States of America — Originality* versus *Imitation, Americanism* versus *Europeanism.*

The Contrast *was the first comedy, written by an American, to be performed in an American theatre, by a company of professional actors.*

*The author of* The Contrast *was Royall Tyler, patriot, poet, wit, dramatist, jurist, born in Boston, Massachusetts, July* 18, 1757, *son of Royall Tyler and Mary (Steele), his wife. His father was a wealthy merchant, a Representative of Boston four years, a King's Councillor from* 1765 *until his death in* 1771, *a member of the Long Room Club and Sons of Liberty, and a lover of religion and literature.*

*Among the memories of Royall Tyler's boyhood were those of the black slaves about the town, and once of a rumor that they would "rise"; of tales told to him of his great-grandfather, the sea-captain, Thomas Tyler, who sailed out of Budleigh, Devonshire, and was lost at sea;*

of the great-uncle Thomas Tyler, captured by Algerine pirates and never heard of again, though large ransom was offered for him; and of the taking of Louisburg by Sir William Pepperell, whose sister Jane was the second wife of his grandfather, the rich merchant, William Tyler; of his father talking about the Mother Country's injustice towards the Colonies; of seeing, as he went to and from the Latin School, handbills posted up warning persons not to use stamped papers; of the Liberty Tree, with effigies hanging on it, and of the bonfires when news of the repeal of the Stamp Act arrived; of British troops landing, marching through the streets and thereafter patrolling them; of hearing shots, bells ringing, the noise of people rushing by the house, shouts, and a hurried call to his father to meet the Governor and Council, the evening of the Boston Massacre, in March, 1770; and of the sudden ending of his happy home life by the deaths of his father and his eldest sister in May, 1771.

Royall Tyler entered college in July, 1772, one of a class many of whom afterwards distinguished themselves. The excitement of the times was reflected in the College Hall, where there was a fracas, one breakfast hour, over the drinking of tea by some of the students, and its non-use was agreed upon. The dispersion of the collegians after the Battle of Lexington until the following October gave Royall Tyler opportunities of association with the officers of the Revolutionary Army, and he may well have seen Washington take command of the Army in Cambridge,

*His only brother was chosen by Washington for hazardous enterprises. Their mother s need of having one son near, in her second widowhood, prevented Royall from entering military service. He graduated from Harvard, July, 1776, with degree of A.B., Yale giving him B.A. in October of the same year;[1] studied law and was one of the group of brilliant young men who met in Colonel John Trumbull's rooms, where " they regaled themselves with a cup of tea, instead of wine, and discussed subjects of literature, politics, and War." Joining the Independent Company of Boston in 1776, he served, as aide with rank of major, under General Sullivan in the campaign against Newport in 1778.*

*Admitted to the bar August 19, 1780, he first practised in Falmouth (now Portland), Maine, later settling in Braintree (now Quincy). Very handsome, with a musical voice, fond of social intercourse, devoted to kindred and friends, fond of children and always ready to amuse them, bubbling over with gaiety and humorous speech, with a keen eye for foibles and a ready tongue for satirizing them, a boyish liking for playing jokes on people, openhearted and generous, he was admired by many and hated by a few. His reputation for wit, scholarship, legal and literary genius was widely extended.*

*Soon he became the ardent lover and accepted suitor of beautiful Miss Abby Adams. When he was on the eve of crossing the seas to wed his betrothed — then in Europe*

[1] *He received the degree of A. M. from Harvard in 1799, and the University of Vermont gave him an honorary degree of A.M. in 1811.*

with her parents — his letters and gifts to her were returned to him, with a verbal message of dismissal.

Being of a sensitive temperament and deep affections, this disappointment was a crushing blow. He shut up his law office, and for several months secluded himself from all his friends in his mother's home in Jamaica Plain; but his character was too vigorous to permit melancholy long to hold him in thrall. Resuming his law practice in Boston in 1785, he boarded with the Honorable Joseph Pearse Palmer and his family. Little "Polly" (Mary) Palmer, an unusually intelligent and lovely child, was a great favorite of his, and, playfully, he used to call her his "little wife."

During Shays's Rebellion, 1786–87, he served as aide to General Lincoln, with rank of major; actively, in the field with a troop of cavalry, and diplomatically, on a mission to the government of Vermont.

From Bennington, under date of February 17, 1787, Major Tyler wrote a hasty note to his friends the Palmers, in Boston, concluding with the words "Love to my little wife." This message was to the child who afterwards became his wife, whose single-hearted affection for Royall Tyler, from the day of their first meeting when she was a very little girl to the end of a long life, has been enshrined in the memories of five generations of descendants.

Sent to New York on a similar mission from Governor Bowdoin to Governor Clinton, he reached there on March 12, 1787, and was immediately introduced to the society and pleasures of the city. He became a constant attendant *at the John Street Theatre, and intimate with the actors, especially with Wignell, the comedian of the American Company.*

*If Major Tyler went to the theatre the evening that he arrived, he witnessed the performance of Addison's* Cato, *and through the month* Richard III, School for Scandal, Jane Shore, Cymbeline, Alexander the Great, *and* The True-Born Irishman.

*Whether the statement of a New York correspondent to a Boston paper under date of April 16, 1887 (the centennial anniversary of the first performance of* The Contrast), *that " Royall Tyler arrived in New York from Boston, bringing with him the unfinished play,' is true, I cannot prove. At that date there were persons living who had been acquainted with* Mrs. Royall Tyler, *and who might have known her husband, and it is possible that the correspondent was transmitting to the public information that he had verbally received. It is certainly to be inferred from a perusal of the unpublished Memoirs of Royall Tyler that, prior to* 1787, *he had been urged by those who believed in his literary powers to try his hand at writing drama, and that, if he did not carry to New York the unfinished play in his pocket, he may have carried the idea in his mind.*

*It is told in family annals that Royall Tyler wrote verse and prose from his college days, but unless the four manuscript poems in the Boston Public Library were written prior to* The Contrast, *this comedy is the earliest of his writings to be preserved. We can imagine the eagerness* with which the manager of the American Company read the manuscript of The Contrast, accepted it, and prepared for its production. A newspaper writer, April 14, 1787, said, " I wait with impatience for the new comedy, for I believe it will supply a great deal of game."

❊❊❊❊❊❊❊❊❊❊❊❊❊❊❊❊❊❊❊❊❊❊❊❊❊❊❊❊❊

## THEATRE — ON THIS EVENING

*Never performed*

(BEING THE 16TH OF APRIL)
will be performed a COMEDY of Five Acts,
written by a CITIZEN *of the* United States,

CALLED

## THE CONTRAST

❊❊❊❊❊❊❊❊❊❊❊❊❊❊❊❊❊❊❊❊❊❊❊❊❊❊❊❊❊

*To which will be added the* ENGLISH BURLETTO
*called* MIDAS

runs the advertisement of the first performance of Royall Tyler s comedy in the New York newspapers of April 16, 1787.

The little John Street Theatre was crowded, April 16, 1787, we can be sure, with rank and fashion. The theatre was of wood, painted red, back some sixty feet from the street, and entered by a rough covered passageway, from street to doors. The performances were arranged so as not to interfere with the evening Assemblies, and were given only two or three times a week. Doors opened at 5.30 and the performance began at 6.15. The duties of the candle-snuffer were no sinecure, as candles gave the only light and needed continual attention. Prices were, for a seat in a box, eight shillings ($1.00); in the pit, six shillings; and in the gallery, four shillings. A full house would total eight hundred dollars. The writer who hoped for " a great deal of game" from the "new comedy,' complains in the same article of the scenery and that "the musicians, instead of performing between the play and farce, are suffered to leave the theatre to pay a visit to the tippling houses, and the ladies, in the meantime, must amuse themselves by looking at the candles and the empty benches" Is the inference to be drawn that the gentlemen in the house followed the example of the musicians?

The Contrast was repeated, April 18, with alterations; May 2, "at the particular request of his excellency, Mr. Hancock"; and May 12, "for the benefit of the unhappy sufferers by the late fire at Boston (at the particular request of the Author)."

May 19, on Mr. Wignell's night, after the play The Recruiting Officer, there was given "A Comic Opera in 2 Acts (never performed) written by the author of The Contrast, called May Day in Town, or New York in an Uproar. The music compiled from the most eminent masters with an overture and accompaniments." The songs of the opera were sold on the evening of the performance. The farce was a skit on May Day as moving-day.

William Grayson (M. C.) writing to Madison, May 24, 1787, from New York, said: "Dear Sir, We have lately had a new farce wrote by Poet Tyler, called May

Day : *It has plott and incident and is as good as several of ye English farces ; It has however not succeeded well, owing I believe to ye author s making his principal character a scold. Some of the New York ladies were alarmed for fear strangers should look upon Mrs. Sanders as the model of the gentlewomen of this place. William Grayson* " [1]

*A composite of quotations from the long critical reviews in the contemporary newspapers shows the public estimate of play and author : "The production of a man of genius ...nothing can be more praiseworthy than the sentiments of the play They are the effusions of an honest, patriot heart expressed with energy and eloquence.... Maria's song and her reflections after it, are pretty but certainly misplaced...the many beauties of the play...the unceasing plaudits of the audience did them ample justice.... Upon the whole the defects of the play are much overbalanced by its merits."*

*"Many of the first characters of the United States were also present The repeated bursts of applause...is the most unequivocal proof of its possessing the true requisites of comedy in a very great degree." It "was performed amid continued roars of applause...an American comic production is a novelty, therefore it was pleasing... the piece had merit...merit, with novelty, forces applause."*

*" That lively effort of American Dramatic Genius, the Comedy of* The Contrast *was represented...to a numerous and brilliant Audience, with reiterated Bursts of Applause, giving a convincing Proof to liberal minds, that*

[1] *Madison Papers, Library of Congress.*

*the* Stage *may justly be styled a* School for rational Instruction and innocent Recreation."

*Once more it was given in New York—June* 10,1789. *Mary Palmer was then living in the family of the Honorable Elbridge Gerry. She has recorded, in an unpublished autobiography, the delight she experienced in hearing Mr. Gerry and his family talking of the success of* The Contrast, *enacting parts of it, and praising the genius of its author in "writing of the Yankee in such a masterly way," and how keenly she disliked their criticisms. She understood "that Charlotte and Jonathan were the favorites" of the public.*

*Philadelphia heard Wignell read* The Contrast *in December,* 1787, *and it was twice performed there, in July,* 1790. *Baltimore saw* The Contrast, *November,* 1787, *and August,* 1788. *A "pirated performance" was given in Williamsburg in* 1791. *In October,* 1792, The Contrast *was brought out in Boston at an experimental theatre recently built, but called an* Exhibition Room, *the plays being called* Moral Lectures, *in deference to the State law against theatrical representations and the weight of prejudice against play-acting "still existent among the people." The last performance of* The Contrast *in the lifetime of its author was in Boston, May,* 1795.

*I wish I could record that Washington witnessed a performance of* The Contrast, *but he did not. He was not in New York in* 1787, *was ill at the time of its revival in* 1789, *and was not in Baltimore, Philadelphia, or Williamsburg when it was given in those cities.*

*Royall Tyler was so delighted with Wignell's acting of* Jonathan *that he gave him the copyright of the play, insisting that his own name should not appear on the title-page.* January, 1790, *Wignell published* The Contrast *in Philadelphia, by subscription. The list of subscribers was headed by "The President of the United States." Wignell gave two beautifully bound copies to the President and received his acknowledgment of the gift. One of Washington s copies of* The Contrast *is owned by Mr. James B. Wilbur, of Manchester, Vermont. It is considered one of the best examples of American bookbinding.*

*The authorship of the song sung by Maria, called "very pretty" by a contemporary reviewer, has been in dispute. Mr. McKee, in the Introduction to the Dunlap, 1887, edition of* The Contrast, *expressed the belief that Royall Tyler wrote it.*

The Death Song of a Cherokee Indian *was published in* January, 1787, *in* The American Museum, or Repository of Ancient and Modern Fugitives, *(vol. 1, p. 90,) unsigned. In an edition of* The Museum, 1790, *the song is placed under P. Freneau s name. Philip Freneau, jealous as he was of his literary reputation, never included this song in his printed collections of his works.*

New Spain, or, Love in Mexico, *an opera acted and published in London, 1790, contained the song, with omissions and additions, and it appeared (I am told) in the libretto of* Tammany, *by Mrs. Hatton in 1794.*

*An anthropologist says that the name "Alknomook," with its variations, "Alknomock," as in* The American

Museum *version of* The Death Song of a Cherokee Indian, *and "Alknom*oak," *as in the same song in the opera of* New Spain, *or* Love in New Mexico, *is of Algonquin origin. A New-Englander, writing an Indian song, would naturally use an Algonquin name, as Algonquin Indians inhabited that section of the United States. Royall Tyler published dozens of songs, and his almost invariable custom was to conceal his identity when his writings were printed.*

*Mr. McKee said that "the music was published contemporaneously with the play." A copy of the original sheet music in the New York Public Library, headed* Alknomook, The Death Song of the Cherokee Indians, New York, Printed & sold by G. Gilfert, No 177 Broadway. Likewise to be had of P. A. Van Hagens, Music store, No 3 Cornhill, Boston, *has, in the margin, by the "Library Authorities" the date,* 1800, *with a question-mark, and also the manuscript note, " The New York Directories give George Gilfert's address at* 177 Broadway *from* 1798–1801."

*Mrs. Anne (Home) Hunter, the wife of a celebrated English physician, included* Alknomook, *version as in* The Contrast, *in a volume of* Poems *published in London by T. Payne in* 1802 *and* 1803. *There is a review of these* Poems *mentioning* The Death Song of the Indian, the son of Alknomook, *in the* British Critic, *October,* 1802, *vol.* 20, *p.* 409. *In an obituary notice of Mrs. Hunter occurs this sentence, "* The death song of Alknomook, *the Indian warrior, was written before many of those who sing it now were born...."* (The Gentleman's Magazine, *vol.* 91, *pt.* 1, *January,* 1821, *p.* 90.)

*An English writer says, referring to Mrs. Hunter s Poems, "The 'Death-Song of Alknomook' is there, such a popular song in its day, written for the gentleman who had resided amongst the Cherokee Indians and had sung their wild music in the drawing room at Leicester Square." (From article by Flora Mason in* Blackwood's Magazine, *February,* 1905, *pp.* 217–233, *"Mrs. John Hunter the Surgeon s Wife.")*

*These are the chief facts that I have been able to discover in regard to Maria's song.*

*That* The Contrast *largely aided in dissolving the prejudice against the theatre cannot be gainsaid.*

*Sheridan s* School for Scandal *no doubt served as a model for the inexperienced dramatist, who had not been inside a regular theatre before coming to New York, but* The Contrast *was truly an* American *comedy, a crystallization, clothed and endowed with life, of* the contrasts *of the tastes and fashions, the manners and morals, of the period.*

*The play was an illustrated lesson in patriotism needed, because, mingling with stanch patriots, were those who aped foreign modes and felt, or feigned to feel, disdain for the new Republic and distrust of its Government.*

*The creation of* Jonathan *was a stroke of genius — nothing else — a real Yankee, true to type in each word and act, the original of the stage Yankee seen from that day to this. Jonathan s use of the words of* Yankee Doodle *is the first instance of their appearance in a play, though I believe the air is used in Barton's* Disappointment *(1767, not acted). Jonathan's reference to "bundling," then a well-known country custom, was a skilful touch of truthful delineation. "Brother Jonathan" has long stood, in pictures, songs, and stories, as the impersonation of "Uncle Sam," invariably garbed and delineated as a typical Yankee. It seems to me probable that this characterization of "Brother Jonathan" arose from the fusing in the public mind of the popular Yankee Jonathan in* The Contrast *and the general knowledge that Washington often said, when perplexed, "Let us consult Brother Jonathan," meaning the stanch Yankee patriot Jonathan Trumbull, Governor of Connecticut.*

*Royall Tyler was preeminently a patriot in his sentiments, and I believe that in* Manly's *character he expressed himself, disguised by some characteristics not his own.*

The Contrast *was widely read, copies finding their way into remote country districts. An illustration of this is the fact that the author, when on a horseback trip into the State of New York in 1792, found that his host in New Lebanon possessed a well-worn copy and, moreover, knew the play almost by heart.*

*William Dunlap, called "the father of American drama," returning to New York while the success of* The Contrast *was still the talk of the town, was stimulated to emulation and at once began his career, remarkably rewarded, as an American dramatist.*

*Removing to Vermont in 1790, Royall Tyler became a successful advocate and jurist—State's Attorney for Windham County, 1794-1801; Side-Judge, 1801-1807; Chief Justice of the Supreme Court of Vermont, 1807-1813; Trustee (1802-1813) and Professor of Jurisprudence (1811-1814) of the University of Vermont; after leaving the Bench, Register of Probate for Windham County for six years. He died in Brattleboro, Vermont, after five years of severe disease, nobly endured, August 26, 1826.*

*He was noted throughout the State for his strict integrity, his breadth of sympathy, his learning and depth of knowledge of the Law. His personality so stamped itself on the State that, to this day, lawyers know of his ability and genius, and anecdotes of his proceedings in courts and his witty conversation have been handed down among them. His charges were especially valued by the barristers of the day. He was largely instrumental in stabilizing law proceedings and public sentiment in the days when many minds were unsettled and inclined to countenance lawlessness.*

*He was a prolific writer, but his verse and prose, with a few exceptions, were written hastily, as relaxation from the serious business of life, and he rarely polished and pruned his work. His writings in magazines and newspapers deal with contemporary drama and theatrical representations, with the whole range of literature, and with the topics of the day, its shifting fashions, its politics, and its manners and morals. A Federalist in poli-*

tics, he had, at times, a breadth of vision in advance of his age. A Vermont newspaper article printed shortly after his death spoke of him as " one of our most distinguished advocates" and of "that classical eloquence which has given great celebrity to his name," and closed with the following appreciation : "As a man of genius, a poet, an orator, a civilian and erudite and accomplished scholar, and a gentleman of the most elegant and endearing manners in social and domestic life, his memory will long be cherished with affection and respect, by the companions of his youth in Massachusetts, and those of his mature and declining years in Vermont. The Algerine Captive, unquestionably one of the most original and brilliant productions of this generation, will forever secure him a high rank among American writers, and the future admirers of his beautiful poems will ' give his name in charge to the sweet lyre '" (Northern Sentinel, September 8, 1826.)

A glance through the remains of Royall Tyler's wide correspondence affords interesting glimpses of the appreciation of his character felt by the writers. Letters and Journals of himself, wife, and kindred reveal the nobility of spirit, the lovingkindness of heart, the courage of soul that knit him to them in ties of devotion and admiration.

HELEN TYLER BROWN

Brattleboro, Vermont, September, 1920

# THE CONTRAST

## A Comedy in Five Acts

As *a just acknowledgment of the liberal exertions by which the* STAGE *has been rescued from an ignominious proscription*

# THE CONTRAST

*(being the first essay of American Genius in the dramatic art) is most respectfully dedicated to the President and Members of the Dramatic Association by their most obliged and most grateful servant*

THOMAS WIGNELL

{ PHILADELPHIA }
{ 1 *January*, 1790 }

# ADVERTISEMENT

THE *Subscribers (to whom the Editor thankfully professes his obligations) may reasonably expect an apology for the delay which has attended the appearance of* THE CONTRAST; *but, as the true cause cannot be declared without leading to a discussion, which the Editor wishes to avoid, he hopes that the care and expense which have been bestowed upon this work will be accepted, without further scrutiny, as an atonement for his seeming negligence.*

*In justice to the Author, however, it may be proper to observe that this Comedy has many claims to the public indulgence, independent of its intrinsic merits: It is the first essay of American genius in a difficult species of composition; it was written by one who never critically studied the rules of the drama, and, indeed, had seen but few of the exhibitions of the stage; it was undertaken and finished in the course of three weeks; and the profits of one night's performance were appropriated to the benefit of the sufferers by the fire at Boston.*

*These considerations will, therefore, it is hoped, supply in the closet the advantages that are derived from representation, and dispose the reader to join in the applause which has been bestowed upon this Comedy by numerous and judicious audiences, in the Theatres of Philadelphia, New-York, and Maryland.*

# LIST OF SUBSCRIBERS

THE PRESIDENT of the United States.

## A

Roger Alden, Esq., New-York, 2 copies.
Samuel Anderson, Esq.
Mr. Henry Anderson.
Mr. George Arnold.

Mr. W. Alexander, Philadelphia.
Mr. Joseph Anthony.
Mr. Thomas P. Anthony.

Alexander Aikman, Esq., Island of Jamaica, 20 copies.

## B

J. Barrell, Esq., Boston.

Dr. Richard Bayley, New-York.
William Banyer, Esq.
Mr. George N. Bleecker.
George Bond, Esq.
Mr. Samuel Bowne.
Mr. Michael Boyle.
Mr. Laban Bronson.
Aaron Burr, Esq.

William Bingham, Esq., Philadelphia, 2 copies.
John Bernard, Esq.
Mr. Thomas Bell.
Mr. Joseph Bell.
Mr. Charles Biddle.
Mr. William Blake.

Mr. Nathan Boys, Philadelphia.
Mr. Hugh Boyle.
Daniel Broadhead, Esq.
James Bryson, Esq.
Mr. Thomas Bradford, 12 copies.
Mr. John Brown.
Mr. William Brown.
Mr. William Brown.
Mr. Richard Brown.
William-Ward Burrows, Esq.

Honorable James Brice, Maryland, 2 copies.
Mr. Mathew Beard.
Mr. John Beard.
Mr. Thomas Bicknell.
Fielder Bowie, Esq., 2 copies.
Captain Bright.
Major William Brogden, 2 copies.
Mr. Arthur Bryan.
Mr. Nicholas Brewer.
John Bullen, Esq., 2 copies.

P. Bowdoin, Esq., Virginia.
Mr. John Brooks.
Mr. Daniel Broadhead.

John Beard, Esq., London.

## C

Charles Van Cortlant, Esq., New-York.

Mr. David C. Claypoole, Philadelphia.
Mr. Richard Moses Clegg.
Tench Coxe, Esq.
Mr. James Crawford.

Honorable Charles Carroll, Maryland, 6 copies.
Nicholas Carroll, Esq., 6 copies.
James Carroll, Esq., 6 copies.

# LIST OF SUBSCRIBERS

John Callahan, Esq., Maryland, 3 copies.
William Campbell, Esq., 6 copies.
Mr. Walter Chandler.
Mr. Joseph Clark, 6 copies.
Mr. Stephen Clark (bookseller), 7 copies.
Mr. Abraham Claude.
Mr. James Cowan.
Miss Mary Cummins.

Paul Carrington, Esq., Virginia.
Mr. Roger Chew.
Mr. George Coryell.
Mr. Richard Conway.
Mr. Samuel Craig.
Mr. James Craik.

Mathew Coulthurst, Esq., Barbadoes.

## D

Mr. William Dunlap, New-York.

A. J. Dallas, Esq., Philadelphia.
Mrs. Dallas.
Mr. James Davidson, jun.
Mr. Thomas Dobson, 6 copies.
Mr. John Dorsey.
Capt. Patrick Duffey.
Mr. John Dunkin.
Mr. John Dunlap.
A Friend to the Drama.
A Friend to the Drama.

Honorable Major Davidson, Maryland, 4 copies.
John Davidson, Esq., 2 copies.
Mrs. Eleanor Davidson, 3 copies.
Capt. Robert Denny, 2 copies.
George Dent, Esq.
George Digges, Esq., 6 copies.

Mr. Isaac Dorsey, Maryland.
Gabriel Duvall, Esq., 2 copies.

Mr. John B. Dabney, Virginia.
Mr. Robert Donaldson.

P. M. Drummond, Esq., Madeira.

## E

W. Edgar, Esq., New-York.
John Charles Evans, Esq.

Marcus Elean, Esq., Virginia.

## F

Mr. George Fox, Philadelphia.
William-Temple Franklin, Esq.
William Fousher, Esq.
Mr. Alexander Fullerton.

William Fitzhugh, jun., Esq., Maryland, 2 copies.
Mr. Ralph Forster, 2 copies.
Mr. William Foxcroft, 2 copies.
Alexander Frazier, Esq., 3 copies.

Mr. William Faulkener, Virginia.
Colonel John Fitzgerald.

Peter Freneau, Esq., Charleston, South Carolina.

## G

Mr. Hugh Gaine, New-York, 12 copies.
Mr. A. Gilet.
Mr. Isaac Gomez, jun.

Mr. Thomas Giese, Philadelphia.
Mr. Charles Gilchrist.
Mr. John Gordon.

John Gale, Esq., Maryland, 2 copies.
Mr. David Geddis.

Capt. John Gassaway, Maryland.
Mr. Charles Grahame, 2 copies.
John Grahame, Esq., 4 copies.
Messrs. Frederick and Samuel Green, 6 copies.
Mr. John Guyer.

William S. Grayson, Esq., Virginia.
Mr. Joseph Greenway.
Mr. Job Greene.

## H

David Van Horne, Esq., New-York.
Colonel David Humphreys.

Mr. Parry Hall, Philadelphia.
William Hamilton, Esq.
Mr. Joseph Harper.
Mr. James Hawthorne.
Mr. R. Hiltzheimer.
Samuel Hodgdon, Esq.
Mr. John Hubley.
George Hughes, Esq.
Asheton Humphreys, Esq.
Mr. Pearson Hunt.

Benjamin Hall, Esq., Maryland, 3 copies.
Capt. John Hamilton, 4 copies.
Mrs. Rebecca Hanson.
William Harwood, Esq., 2 copies.
Honorable Robert-Hanson Harrison, 2 copies.
Nicholas Harwood, Esq.
Thomas Harwood, Esq., 2 copies.
Benjamin Harwood, Esq., 6 copies.
Richard Harwood, jun., Esq.
Mrs. Rachel Harwood.
Mr. Osborn Harwood.
Mr. George R. Hayward, 3 copies.
William Hayward, jun., Esq.

Honorable William Hemsley, Maryland, 2 copies.
Rev. Ralph Higginbotham, 3 copies.
Capt. Philip Hill.
James Hindman, Esq., 2 copies.
Mr. Benjamin Howard.
Mr. Samuel-Harvey Howard, 3 copies.
Mrs. Mary Howard.

Mr. Benjamin A. Hamp, Virginia.
Mr. Nicholas Hannah.
Mr. S. Hanson, of Samuel.
Benjamin Harrison, jun., Esq.
Mr. Gilbert Harrow.
Mr. W. Hodson.
Mr. Charles P. Howard.
Mr. William Hunter, sen.
Mr. William Hunter, jun., Esq.

Mr. Thomas Hall, Charleston, 2 copies.

Thomas Hull, Esq., London.

## I

Honorable H. Izard, New-York.
Mr. John Johnson.

Major W. Jackson, Philadelphia.
Jeremiah Jackson, Esq.

Thomas Jennings, Esq., Maryland, 2 copies.
Mr. Thomas Jennings, jun.
Mr. George Jennings.
Thomas Johnson, jun., Esq., 3 copies.
Mr. Robert Johnson.
Mr. John Johnson.
Mr. Robert Isabel.

Mr. Crawford Jenckes, Virginia.
Mr. C. Jones.

## K

H. Knox, Esq., Secretary of War for the United States, New-York.

Capt. Francis Knox, Philadelphia.
Mr. William Kidd.

Honorable John Kilty, Maryland, 3 copies.
William Kilty, Esq., 3 copies.
Mr. William King.
Miss Eliza Knapp.
Miss Anne Knapp.

Messrs. Warington and Keen, Virginia.
Mr. James Kennedy.

## L

Tobias Lear, Esq., New-York.
William S. Livingston, Esq.
Mr. Samuel Low.

Mr. Thomas Lea, Philadelphia.
William Lewis, Esq., 3 copies.
Mr. William Levis.
Mr. H. I. Lombart.

Honble. Randolph B. Latimer, Maryland, 4 copies.
Benjamin Lowndes, Esq., 2 copies.

Mr. John Lester, Virginia.
Mr. W. Lowrey.

## M

Mr. A. Marshall, New-York.
Mr. Patrick M'Davitt.
Mr. Peter Maverick.
Mr. John Miller.
Jacob Morton, Esq.

His Excellency Thomas Mifflin, President of the State of Pennsylvania, Philadelphia.

Honorable Thomas M'Kean, Chief Justice, Philadelphia.
Honorable Robert Morris.
Stephen Moylan, Esq.
Major Thomas L. Moore.
Mr. William Moore.
Major Mathew M'Connell.
Mr. Owen Morris.
Mr. Peter Markoe.
Mr. John M'Cree.
Mr. James Muir.

Mr. Charles Maccubbin, Maryland, 3 copies.
Mr. James Maccubbin.
Mr. Samuel Maccubbin.
William H. M'Pherson, Esq.
Mrs. Elizabeth M'Pherson.
Mr. Cornelius Mills, 3 copies.
Mr. Robert Miller, 2 copies.
Addison Murdock, Esq., 3 copies.
Dr. James Murray, 2 copies.
John Muir, Esq., 8 copies.
Mr. James M'Culloch.
Mr. Walker Muse.

Mr. P. Marsteller, Virginia.
Mr. John. M'Clenachan.
Mr. Evan M'Clean.
Mr. Joshua Merryman.
Mr. William Miller.
Mr. William M'Whir.
Mr. John Murray.
Mr. Patrick Murray.

Alexander M'Kinnon, Esq., London.

## N

Captain Robert North, Poughkeepsie.

Mr. William Nixon, New-York.

## O

Abraham Ogden, Esq., New-York.
Abraham Osgood, Esq.
Mr. Henry Oudenarde.

Mr. Benjamin Oden, Maryland.
Mrs. B. Ogle, 2 copies.
Mr. Thomas Orrick.
Mr. Richard Owens.

## P

Richard Platt, Esq., New-York, 10 copies.
G. Pintard, Esq., 4 copies.
Mr. George Pollock.
Mr. J. W. Prevost.
William Popham, Esq.

Robert Patton, Esq., Philadelphia.
Charles Pettit, Esq.
Frederick Phile, Esq.
Samuel Powell, Esq.
Mr. William Prichard, 6 copies.
Mrs. Prichard.

Honorable William Paca, Maryland, 6 copies.
Archibald Patison, Esq., 6 copies.
Honorable George Plater, 6 copies.
Mr. John Petty.
Miss Ann Pinckney.
Jonathan Pinckney, jun.
Mr. John R. Plater, 2 copies.
Mr. Thomas Pryse.
Mr. Thomas Purdy.

Mr. William Page, Virginia, 2 copies.
Mr. Henry Peterson.
Mr. John S. Pleasants.

Mr. Thomas Porter, Virginia.
Mr. R. Prucott.

## Q

Allen Quynn, Esq., Maryland, 4 copies.
Mr. Allen Quynn, jun.

## R

Messrs. Berry and Rogers, New-York, 12 copies.
Nicholas G. Rutgers, Esq.

Dr. Joseph Redman, Philadelphia.
Mr. James Rees.
Mr. A. Reinagle.
Mr. John Reed.
Messrs. H. Rice and Co., 6 copies.
Mr. Cropley Rose.

Mr. John Randall, Maryland.
Capt. Philip Reed.
Mr. Simon Retalick.
Christopher Richmond, Esq., 6 copies.
Mr. Paul Richards.
Mr. Samuel Ridout.
Mr. James Ringold.
Mrs. Ringold.
Honorable John Rogers, Esq.

Edmund Randolph, Esq., Attorney-General to the United States;
    Virginia.
Mr. George Richards, 6 copies.
Mr. A. Robb.
Mr. J. Roberdeau.

John Richards, Esq., R.A., London.
Mr. John Robinson.

## S

Major General Baron Stuben, New-York.
Mr. Joseph Sands.

Mr. Henry Saidler, New-York.
Mr. John Sherred.
William S. Smith, Esq.
Mr. George Storer.

General Walter Stewart, Philadelphia.
Mr. Thomas Seddon, 6 copies.
Doctor William Shippen, jun.
William S. Smith, Esq.
Mr. William Spotswood, 6 copies.
Mr. Andrew Spence.
William Steinsen, Esq.

Major Jonathan Sellman, Maryland, 2 copies.
Hugh Sherwood, Esq., 2 copies.
James Shaw, Esq., 4 copies.
Mr. John Shaw, 2 copies.
Doctor John T. Shaaf.
Doctor Clement Smith.
William Smallwood, Esq., late Governor of Maryland, 6 copies.
Mr. Richard Sprigg, jun.
Michael Stone, Esq., 2 copies.
Captain John Stewart.
Doctor James Stewart, 4 copies.
Mr. David Stewart, 2 copies.
Mr. David Stewart, of Doden.

Mr. Robert Sanford, Virginia.
Mr. Charles Simms.
Mr. P. Southall.

## T

Isaiah Thomas, Esq., Massachusetts, 12 copies.

Jonathan Trumbull, Esq., New-York.

Mr. Henry Toland, Philadelphia.
Mr. James Thompson, 2 copies.

John Taylor, Esq., Maryland.

Mr. Benjamin Taylor, Maryland.
John Allen Thomas, Esq., 6 copies.
Mr. Jasper E. Tilley.
Mr. Richard Tootel.
Captain John Trueman.

Mr. Jonah Thompson, Virginia.
St. George Tucker, Esq.

## W

Mr. Richard Ward, New-York.
Honorable Jeremiah Wadsworth, Esq., 6 copies.
Mr. John Wallace.
Mr. Prosper Wetmore.
General S. B. Webb.
Charles Wilkes, Esq.

Mr. George Westcott, Philadelphia.
Honorable James Wilson, Esq.
Mr. Seth Willis.
Mr. William Woodhouse, 6 copies.
Mr. Balthazer Wouters.
Mr. James Withy.

Mr. Nicholas Watkins, Maryland.
Mrs. Catharine Wallace.
Mr. Richard Wells.
Mr. William Wells.
Mr. Joseph Williams.
Mr. William Whetcroft.
Mr. Burton Whetcroft.
Mrs. Rebecca White.
Miss Letitia Whetcroft.
John White, Esq., 4 copies.
Mrs. Frances Whetcroft.
Mr. Brice I. Worthington.
Mr. John G. Worthington, 2 copies.
Mr. Henry Woodcock, 2 copies.

Mr. John Wright, Maryland, 3 copies.

Mr. William Ward, Virginia.
Mr. George A. Washington.
Joseph Westmore, Esq.
Mr. Roger West.


## Y

Hamilton Young, Esq., New-York.

Mr. John Young, Philadelphia.

Mr. Vachel Yates, Maryland.

# PROLOGUE

WRITTEN BY A YOUNG GENTLEMAN OF NEW-YORK, AND SPOKEN BY
MR. WIGNELL

EXULT, each patriot heart! — this night is shewn
A piece, which we may fairly call our own;
Where the proud titles of " My Lord ! Your Grace!"
To humble *Mr.* and plain *Sir* give place.
Our Author pictures not from foreign climes
The fashions or the follies of the times;
But has confin'd the subject of his work
To the gay scenes — the circles of New-York.
On native themes his Muse displays her pow'rs;
If ours the faults, the virtues too are ours.
Why should our thoughts to distant countries roam,
When each refinement may be found at home?
Who travels now to ape the rich or great,
To deck an equipage and roll in state;
To court the graces, or to dance with ease,
Or by hypocrisy to strive to please?
Our free-born ancestors such arts despis'd;
Genuine sincerity alone they priz'd;
Their minds, with honest emulation fir'd;
To solid good — not ornament — aspir'd;
Or, if ambition rous'd a bolder flame,
Stern virtue throve, where indolence was shame.

But modern youths, with imitative sense,
Deem taste in dress the proof of excellence;
And spurn the meanness of your homespun arts,
Since homespun habits would obscure their parts;
Whilst all, which aims at splendour and parade,
Must come from Europe, *and be ready made.*

Strange! we should thus our native worth disclaim,
And check the progress of our rising fame.
Yet *one*, whilst imitation bears the sway,
Aspires to nobler heights, and points the way.
Be rous'd, my friends ! his bold example view ;
Let your own Bards be proud to copy *you !*
Should rigid critics reprobate our play,
At least the patriotic heart will say,
" Glorious our fall, since in a noble cause.
" The bold *attempt alone* demands applause.''
Still may the wisdom of the Comic Muse
Exalt your merits, or your faults accuse.
But think not, 't is her aim to be severe ; ——
We all are mortals, and as mortals err.
If candour pleases, we are truly blest ;
Vice trembles, when compell'd to stand confess'd.
Let not light Censure on your faults offend,
Which aims not to expose them, but amend.
Thus does our Author to your candour trust ;
Conscious, the *free* are generous, as just.

# CHARACTERS

| | New-York | Maryland |
|---|---|---|
| Col. Manly | Mr. Henry | Mr. Hallam |
| Dimple | Mr. Hallam | Mr. Harper |
| Van Rough | Mr. Morris | Mr. Morris |
| Jessamy | Mr. Harper | Mr. Biddle |
| Jonathan | Mr. Wignell | Mr. Wignell |
| | | |
| Charlotte | Mrs. Morris | Mrs. Morris |
| Maria | Mrs. Harper | Mrs. Harper |
| Letitia | Mrs. Kenna | Mrs. Williamson |
| Jenny | Miss Tuke | Miss W. Tuke |

SERVANTS

SCENE, *NEW-YORK*

# THE CONTRAST

## ACT I

*Scene, an Apartment at* CHARLOTTE'S

CHARLOTTE *and* LETITIA *discovered*

LETITIA. And so, Charlotte, you really think the pocket-hoop unbecoming.

CHARLOTTE. No, I don't say so. It may be very becoming to saunter round the house of a rainy day; to visit my grand-mamma, or to go to Quakers' meeting: but to swim in a minuet, with the eyes of fifty well-dressed beaux upon me, to trip it in the Mall, or walk on the battery, give me the luxurious, jaunty, flowing, bell-hoop. It would have delighted you to have seen me the last evening, my charming girl! I was dangling o'er the battery with Billy Dimple; a knot of young fellows were upon the platform; as I passed them I faultered with one of the most bewitching false steps you ever saw, and then recovered myself with such a pretty confusion, flirting my hoop to discover a jet black shoe and brilliant buckle. Gad! how my little heart thrilled to hear the confused raptures of — "*Demme, Jack, what a delicate foot!*" "*Ha! General, what a well-turned          *"

LETITIA. Fie! fie! Charlotte [*stopping her mouth*], I protest you are quite a libertine.

CHARLOTTE. Why, my dear little prude, are we not all such libertines? Do you think, when I sat tortured two hours under the hands of my friseur, and an hour more at my toilet, that I had any thoughts of my aunt Susan, or my cousin Betsey? though they are both allowed to be critical judges of dress.

LETITIA. Why, who should we dress to please, but those who are judges of its merit?

CHARLOTTE. Why, a creature who does not know *Buffon* from *Souflee* — Man! — my Letitia — Man! for whom we dress, walk, dance, talk, lisp, languish, and smile. Does not the grave Spectator assure us that even our much bepraised diffidence, modesty, and blushes are all directed to make ourselves good wives and mothers as fast as we can? Why, I'll undertake with one flirt of this hoop to bring more beaux to my feet in one week than the grave Maria, and her sentimental circle, can do, by sighing sentiment till their hairs are grey.

LETITIA. Well, I won't argue with you; you always out-talk me; let us change the subject. I hear that Mr. Dimple and Maria are soon to be married.

CHARLOTTE. You hear true. I was consulted in the choice of the wedding clothes. She is to be married in a delicate white sattin, and has a monstrous pretty brocaded lutestring for the second day. It would have done you good to have seen with what an affected indifference the dear sentimentalist turned over a thousand pretty things, just as if her heart did not palpitate with her approaching happiness, and at last made her choice and arranged her dress with such apathy as if she did not know that plain white sattin and a simple blond lace would shew her clear skin and dark hair to the greatest advantage.

LETITIA. But they say her indifference to dress, and even to the gentleman himself, is not entirely affected.

CHARLOTTE. How?

LETITIA. It is whispered that if Maria gives her hand to Mr. Dimple, it will be without her heart.

CHARLOTTE. Though the giving the heart is one of the last of all laughable considerations in the mar-riage of a girl of spirit, yet I should like to hear what antiquated notions the dear little piece of old-fash-ioned prudery has got in her head.

LETITIA. Why, you know that old Mr. John-Richard-Robert-Jacob-Isaac-Abraham-Cornelius Van Dumpling, Billy Dimple's father (for he has thought fit to soften his name, as well as manners, during his English tour), was the most intimate friend of Maria's father. The old folks, about a year before Mr. Van Dumpling's death, proposed this match: the young folks were accordingly introduced, and told they must love one another. Billy was then a good-natured, decent-dressing young fellow, with a little dash of the coxcomb, such as our young fellows of fortune usually have. At this time, I really believe she thought she loved him; and had they then been married, I doubt not they might have jogged on, to the end of the chapter, a good kind of a sing-song lack-a-daysaical life, as other honest married folks do.

CHARLOTTE. Why did they not then marry?

LETITIA. Upon the death of his father, Billy went to England to see the world and rub off a little of the patroon rust. During his absence, Maria, like a good girl, to keep herself constant to her *nown true-love*, avoided company, and betook herself, for her amuse-ment, to her books, and her dear Billy's letters. But, alas! how many ways has the mischievous demon of inconstancy of stealing into a woman's heart! Her love was destroyed by the very means she took to sup-port it.

CHARLOTTE. How? — Oh! I have it — some likely young beau found the way to her study.

LETITIA. Be patient, Charlotte; your head so runs upon beaux. Why, she read Sir Charles Grandison, Clarissa Harlow, Shenstone, and the Sentimental Journey; and between whiles, as I said, Billy's let-ters. But, as her taste improved, her love declined.

The contrast was so striking betwixt the good sense of her books and the flimsiness of her love/letters, that she discovered she had unthinkingly engaged her hand without her heart; and then the whole transaction, managed by the old folks, now appeared so unsentimental, and looked so like bargaining for a bale of goods, that she found she ought to have rejected, according to every rule of romance, even the man of her choice, if imposed upon her in that manner. Clary Harlow would have scorned such a match.

CHARLOTTE. Well, how was it on Mr. Dimple's return? Did he meet a more favourable reception than his letters?

LETITIA. Much the same. She spoke of him with respect abroad, and with contempt in her closet. She watched his conduct and conversation, and found that he had by travelling acquired the wickedness of Lovelace without his wit, and the politeness of Sir Charles Grandison without his generosity. The ruddy youth, who washed his face at the cistern every morn/ing, and swore and looked eternal love and constancy, was now metamorphosed into a flippant, palid, polite beau, who devotes the morning to his toilet, reads a few pages of Chesterfield's letters, and then minces out, to put the infamous principles in practice upon every woman he meets.

CHARLOTTE. But, if she is so apt at conjuring up these sentimental bugbears, why does she not discard him at once?

LETITIA. Why, she thinks her word too sacred to be trifled with. Besides, her father, who has a great respect for the memory of his deceased friend, is ever telling her how he shall renew his years in their union, and repeating the dying injunctions of old Van Dumpling.

CHARLOTTE. A mighty pretty story! And so you would make me believe that the sensible Maria would give up Dumpling manor, and the all-accomplished Dimple as a husband, for the absurd, ridiculous reason, forsooth, because she despises and abhors him. Just as if a lady could not be privileged to spend a man's fortune, ride in his carriage, be called after his name, and call him her *nown dear lovee* when she wants money, without loving and respecting the great he-creature. Oh! my dear girl, you are a monstrous prude.

LETITIA. I don't say what I would do; I only intimate how I suppose she wishes to act.

CHARLOTTE. No, no, no! A fig for sentiment. If she breaks, or wishes to break, with Mr. Dimple, depend upon it, she has some other man in her eye. A woman rarely discards one lover until she is sure of another. Letitia little thinks what a clue I have to

Dimple's conduct. The generous man submits to render himself disgusting to Maria, in order that she may leave him at liberty to address me. I must change the subject.          [*Aside, and rings a bell.*

*Enter* SERVANT

Frank, order the horses to. —— Talking of marriage, did you hear that Sally Bloomsbury is going to be married next week to Mr. Indigo, the rich Carolinian?

LETITIA. Sally Bloomsbury married! — why, she is not yet in her teens.

CHARLOTTE. I do not know how that is, but you may depend upon it, 'tis a done affair. I have it from the best authority. There is my aunt Wyerly's Hannah. You know Hannah; though a black, she is a wench that was never caught in a lie in her life. Now, Hannah has a brother who courts Sarah, Mrs. Catgut the milliner's girl, and she told Hannah's brother, and Hannah, who, as I said before, is a girl of undoubted veracity, told it directly to me, that Mrs. Catgut was making a new cap for Miss Bloomsbury, which, as it was very dressy, it is very probable is designed for a wedding cap. Now, as she is to be married, who can it be but to Mr. Indigo? Why, there is no other gentleman that visits at her papa's.

LETITIA. Say not a word more, Charlotte. Your

intelligence is so direct and well grounded, it is almost a pity that it is not a piece of scandal.

CHARLOTTE. Oh! I am the pink of prudence. Though I cannot charge myself with ever having discredited a tea-party by my silence, yet I take care never to report anything of my acquaintance, especially if it is to their credit,—*discredit*, I mean,— until I have searched to the bottom of it. It is true, there is infinite pleasure in this charitable pursuit. Oh! how delicious to go and condole with the friends of some backsliding sister, or to retire with some old dowager or maiden aunt of the family, who love scandal so well that they cannot forbear gratifying their appetite at the expense of the reputation of their nearest relations! And then to return full fraught with a rich collection of circumstances, to retail to the next circle of our acquaintance under the strongest injunctions of secrecy,—ha, ha, ha!—interlarding the melancholy tale with so many doleful shakes of the head, and more doleful "Ah! who would have thought it! so amiable, so prudent a young lady, as we all thought her, what a monstrous pity! well, I have nothing to charge myself with; I acted the part of a friend, I warned her of the principles of that rake, I told her what would be the consequence; I told her so, I told her so."—Ha, ha, ha!

LETITIA. Ha, ha, ha! Well, but, Charlotte, you

don't tell me what you think of Miss Bloomsbury's match.

CHARLOTTE. Think! why I think it is probable she cried for a plaything, and they have given her a husband. Well, well, well, the puling chit shall not be deprived of her plaything: 'tis only exchanging London dolls for American babies. — Apropos, of babies, have you heard what Mrs. Affable's high-flying notions of delicacy have come to?

LETITIA. Who, she that was Miss Lovely?

CHARLOTTE. The same; she married Bob Affable of Schenectady. Don't you remember?

*Enter* SERVANT

SERVANT. Madam, the carriage is ready.

LETITIA. Shall we go to the stores first, or visit-ing?

CHARLOTTE. I should think it rather too early to visit, especially Mrs. Prim; you know she is so par-ticular.

LETITIA. Well, but what of Mrs. Affable?

CHARLOTTE. Oh, I'll tell you as we go; come, come, let us hasten. I hear Mrs. Catgut has some of the prettiest caps arrived you ever saw. I shall die if I have not the first sight of them.     [*Exeunt*.

## SCENE II

*A Room in* VAN ROUGH's *House*

MARIA *sitting disconsolate at a Table, with Books,* &c.

SONG

I

The sun sets in night, and the stars shun the day;
But glory remains when their lights fade away!
Begin, ye tormentors! your threats are in vain,
For the son of Alknomook shall never complain.

II

Remember the arrows he shot from his bow;
Remember your chiefs by his hatchet laid low:
Why so slow? — do you wait till I shrink from the pain?
No — the son of Alknomook will never complain.

III

Remember the wood where in ambush we lay,
And the scalps which we bore from your nation away:
Now the flame rises fast, you exult in my pain;
But the son of Alknomook can never complain.

IV

I go to the land where my father is gone;
His ghost shall rejoice in the fame of his son:
Death comes like a friend, he relieves me from pain;
And thy son, Oh Alknomook! has scorn'd to complain.

There is something in this song which ever calls
forth my affections. The manly virtue of courage,
that fortitude which steels the heart against the keen-
est misfortunes, which interweaves the laurel of glory
amidst the instruments of torture and death, displays

something so noble, so exalted, that in despite of the prejudices of education I cannot but admire it, even in a savage. The prepossession which our sex is supposed to entertain for the character of a soldier is, I know, a standing piece of raillery among the wits. A cockade, a lapell'd coat, and a feather, they will tell you, are irresistible by a female heart. Let it be so. Who is it that considers the helpless situation of our sex, that does not see that we each moment stand in need of a protector, and that a brave one too? Formed of the more delicate materials of nature, endowed only with the softer passions, incapable, from our ignorance of the world, to guard against the wiles of mankind, our security for happiness often depends upon their generosity and courage. Alas! how little of the former do we find! How inconsistent! that man should be leagued to destroy that honour upon which solely rests his respect and esteem. Ten thousand temptations allure us, ten thousand passions betray us; yet the smallest deviation from the path of rectitude is followed by the contempt and insult of man, and the more remorseless pity of woman; years of penitence and tears cannot wash away the stain, nor a life of virtue obliterate its remembrance. Reputation is the life of woman; yet courage to protect it is masculine and disgusting; and the only safe asylum a woman of delicacy can find is in the arms of a

man of honour. How naturally, then, should we love
the brave and the generous; how gratefully should we
bless the arm raised for our protection, when nerv'd
by virtue and directed by honour! Heaven grant that
the man with whom I may be connected— may be
connected! Whither has my imagination transported
me—whither does it now lead me? Am I not indissolubly engaged, "by every obligation of honour
which my own consent and my father's approbation
can give," to a man who can never share my affections, and whom a few days hence it will be criminal for
me to disapprove—to disapprove! would to heaven
that were all— to despise. For, can the most frivo-
lous manners, actuated by the most depraved heart,
meet, or merit, anything but contempt from every
woman of delicacy and sentiment?

[VAN ROUGH *without.* Mary!]

Ha! my father's voice— Sir!——

*Enter* VAN ROUGH

VAN ROUGH. What, Mary, always singing doleful
ditties, and moping over these plaguy books.

MARIA. I hope, Sir, that it is not criminal to improve my mind with books, or to divert my melancholy with singing, at my leisure hours.

VAN ROUGH. Why, I don't know that, child; I
don't know that. They us'd to say, when I was a

young man, that if a woman knew how to make a pudding, and to keep|herself out of fire and water, she knew enough for a wife. Now, what good have these books done you? have they not made you melancholy? as you call it. Pray, what right has a girl of your age to be in the dumps? haven't you everything your heart can wish; an't you going to be married to a young man of great fortune; an't you going to have the quit-rent of twenty miles square?

MARIA. One-hundredth part of the land, and a lease for life of the heart of a man I could love, would satisfy me.

VAN ROUGH. Pho, pho, pho! child; nonsense, downright nonsense, child. This comes of your reading your story-books; your Charles Grandisons, your Sentimental Journals, and your Robinson Crusoes, and such other trumpery. No, no, no! child; it is money makes the mare go; keep your eye upon the main chance, Mary.

MARIA. Marriage, Sir, is, indeed, a very serious affair.

VAN ROUGH. You are right, child; you are right. I am sure I found it so, to my cost.

MARIA. I mean, Sir, that as marriage is a portion for life, and so intimately involves our happiness, we cannot be too considerate in the choice of our companion.

VAN ROUGH. Right, child; very right. A young woman should be very sober when she is making her choice, but when she has once made it, as you have done, I don't see why she should not be as merry as a grig; I am sure she has reason enough to be so. Solomon says that "there is a time to laugh, and a time to weep." Now, a time for a young woman to laugh is when she has made sure of a good rich husband. Now, a time to cry, according to you, Mary, is when she is making choice of him; but I should think that a young woman's time to cry was when she despaired of *getting* one. Why, there was your mother, now: to be sure, when I popp'd the question to her she did look a little silly; but when she had once looked down on her apron-strings, as all modest young women us'd to do, and drawled out ye–s, she was as brisk and as merry as a bee.

MARIA. My honoured mother, Sir, had no motive to melancholy; she married the man of her choice.

VAN ROUGH. The man of her choice! And pray, Mary, an't you going to marry the man of your choice—what trumpery notion is this? It is these vile books [*throwing them away*]. I'd have you to know, Mary, if you won't make young Van Dumpling the man of *your* choice, you shall marry him as the man of *my* choice.

MARIA. You terrify me, Sir. Indeed, Sir, I am all submission. My will is yours.

VAN ROUGH. Why, that is the way your mother us'd to talk. "My will is yours, my dear Mr. Van Rough, my will is yours"; but she took special care to have her own way, though, for all that.

MARIA. Do not reflect upon my mother's memory, Sir ——

VAN ROUGH. Why not, Mary, why not? She kept me from speaking my mind all her *life*, and do you think she shall henpeck me now she is *dead* too? Come, come; don't go to sniveling; be a good girl, and mind the main chance. I'll see you well settled in the world.

MARIA. I do not doubt your love, Sir, and it is my duty to obey you. I will endeavour to make my duty and inclination go hand in hand.

VAN ROUGH. Well, well, Mary; do you be a good girl, mind the main chance, and never mind inclination. Why, do you know that I have been down in the cellar this very morning to examine a pipe of Madeira which I purchased the week you were born, and mean to tap on your wedding day? —— That pipe cost me fifty pounds sterling. It was well worth sixty pounds; but I overreach'd Ben Bulkhead, the supercargo. I'll tell you the whole story. You must know that ——

*Enter* SERVANT

SERVANT. Sir, Mr. Transfer, the broker, is below.
[*Exit.*

VAN ROUGH. Well, Mary, I must go. Remember, and be a good girl, and mind the main chance.
[*Exit.*

MARIA [*alone*]. How deplorable is my situation! How distressing for a daughter to find her heart militating with her filial duty! I know my father loves me tenderly; why then do I reluctantly obey him? Heaven knows! with what reluctance I should oppose the will of a parent, or set an example of filial disobedience; at a parent's command, I could wed awkwardness and deformity. Were the heart of my husband good, I would so magnify his good qualities with the eye of conjugal affection, that the defects of his person and manners should be lost in the emanation of his virtues. At a father's command, I could embrace poverty. Were the poor man my husband, I would learn resignation to my lot; I would enliven our frugal meal with good humour, and chase away misfortune from our cottage with a smile. At a father's command, I could almost submit to what every female heart knows to be the most mortifying, to marry a weak man, and blush at my husband's folly in every company I visited. But to marry a depraved wretch, whose only virtue is a polished exterior; who is actuated by the unmanly ambition of conquering the defenceless; whose heart, insensible to the emotions of patriotism, dilates at the plaudits of every unthinking girl; whose laurels are the sighs and tears of the miserable victims of his specious behaviour, — can he, who has no regard for the peace and happiness of other families, ever have a due regard for the peace and happiness of his own? Would to heaven that my father were not so hasty in his temper? Surely, if I were to state my reasons for declining this match, he would not compel me to marry a man, whom, though my lips may solemnly promise to honour, I find my heart must ever despise. [*Exit.*

END OF THE FIRST ACT

## ACT II. SCENE I

*Enter* CHARLOTTE *and* LETITIA

CHARLOTTE [*at entering*]. Betty, take those things out of the carriage and carry them to my chamber; see that you don't tumble them. My dear, I protest, I think it was the homeliest of the whole. I declare I was almost tempted to return and change it.

LETITIA. Why would you take it?

CHARLOTTE. Didn't Mrs. Catgut say it was the most fashionable?

LETITIA. But, my dear, it will never fit becomingly on you.

CHARLOTTE. I know that; but did not you hear Mrs. Catgut say it was fashionable?

LETITIA. Did you see that sweet airy cap with the white sprig?

CHARLOTTE. Yes, and I longed to take it; but, my dear, what could I do? Did not Mrs. Catgut say it was the most fashionable; and if I had not taken it, was not that awkward gawky, Sally Slender, ready to purchase it immediately?

LETITIA. Did you observe how she tumbled over the things at the next shop, and then went off without purchasing anything, nor even thanking the poor man for his trouble? But, of all the awkward creatures, did you see Miss Blouze endeavouring to thrust her unmerciful arm into those small kid gloves?

CHARLOTTE. Ha, ha, ha, ha!

LETITIA. Then did you take notice with what an affected warmth of friendship she and Miss Wasp met? when all their acquaintance know how much pleasure they take in abusing each other in every company.

CHARLOTTE. Lud! Letitia, is that so extraordinary? Why, my dear, I hope you are not going to turn sentimentalist. Scandal, you know, is but amusing ourselves with the faults, foibles, follies, and reputations of our friends; indeed, I don t know why we should have friends, if we are not at liberty to make use of them. But no person is so ignorant of the world as to suppose, because I amuse myself with a lady's faults, that I am obliged to quarrel with her person every time we meet: believe me, my dear, we should have very few acquaintance at that rate.

SERVANT *enters and delivers a letter to* CHARLOTTE, *and* ——— [*Exit.*

CHARLOTTE. You'll excuse me, my dear.

[*Opens and reads to herself.*

LETITIA. Oh, quite excusable.

CHARLOTTE. As I hope to be married, my brother Henry is in the city.

LETITIA. What, your brother, Colonel Manly?

CHARLOTTE. Yes, my dear; the only brother I have in the world.

LETITIA. Was he never in this city?

CHARLOTTE. Never nearer than Harlem Heights, where he lay with his regiment.

LETITIA. What sort of a being is this brother of yours? If he is as chatty, as pretty, as sprightly as you, half the belles in the city will be pulling caps for him.

CHARLOTTE. My brother is the very counterpart and reverse of me: I am gay, he is grave; I am airy, he is solid; I am ever selecting the most pleasing objects for my laughter, he has a tear for every pitiful one. And thus, whilst he is plucking the briars and thorns from the path of the unfortunate, I am strewing my own path with roses.

LETITIA. My sweet friend, not quite so poetical, and a little more particular.

CHARLOTTE. Hands off, Letitia. I feel the rage of simile upon me; I can't talk to you in any other way. My brother has a heart replete with the noblest sentiments, but then, it is like — it is like — Oh! you provoking girl, you have deranged all my ideas — it is like — Oh! I have it — his heart is like an old maiden lady's bandbox; it contains many costly things, arranged with the most scrupulous nicety, yet the misfortune is that they are too delicate, costly, and antiquated for common use.

LETITIA. By what I can pick out of your flowery description, your brother is no beau.

CHARLOTTE. No, indeed; he makes no pretension to the character. He'd ride, or rather fly, an hundred miles to relieve a distressed object, or to do a gallant act in the service of his country; but should you drop your fan or bouquet in his presence, it is ten to one that some beau at the farther end of the room would have the honour of presenting it to you before he had observed that it fell. I'll tell you one of his anti-quated, anti-gallant notions. He said once in my pres-ence, in a room full of company, — would you be-lieve it? — in a large circle of ladies, that the best evi-dence a gentleman could give a young lady of his re-spect and affection was to endeavour in a friendly man-ner to rectify her foibles. I protest I was crimson to the eyes, upon reflecting that I was known as his sis-ter.

LETITIA. Insupportable creature! tell a lady of her faults! if he is so grave, I fear I have no chance of captivating him.

CHARLOTTE. His conversation is like a rich, old-fashioned brocade, — it will stand alone; every sen-tence is a sentiment. Now you may judge what a time I had with him, in my twelve months' visit to my

father. He read me such lectures, out of pure brotherly affection, against the extremes of fashion, dress,
flirting, and coquetry, and all the other dear things
which he knows I doat upon, that I protest his conversation made me as melancholy as if I had been at
church; and heaven knows, though I never prayed
to go there but on one occasion, yet I would have ex-
changed his conversation for a psalm and a sermon.
Church is rather melancholy, to be sure; but then I
can ogle the beaux, and be regaled with " here end-
eth the first lesson," but his brotherly *here*, you would
think had no end. You captivate him! Why, my dear,
he would as soon fall in love with a box of Italian flow-
ers. There is Maria, now, if she were not engaged,
she might do something. Oh! how I should like to
see that pair of pensorosos together, looking as grave
as two sailors' wives of a stormy night, with a flow of
sentiment meandering through their conversation
like purling streams in modern poetry.

LETITIA. Oh! my dear fanciful ——

CHARLOTTE. Hush! I hear some person coming
through the entry.

*Enter* SERVANT

SERVANT. Madam, there's a gentleman below who
calls himself Colonel Manly; do you chuse to be at
home?

CHARLOTTE. Shew him in. [*Exit Servant.*] Now for a sober face.

*Enter* COLONEL MANLY

MANLY. My dear Charlotte, I am happy that I once more enfold you within the arms of fraternal affection. I know you are going to ask (amiable impatience!) how our parents do, — the venerable pair transmit you their blessing by me. They totter on the verge of a well-spent life, and wish only to see their children settled in the world, to depart in peace.

CHARLOTTE. I am very happy to hear that they are well. [*Coolly.*] Brother, will you give me leave to introduce you to our uncle's ward, one of my most intimate friends?

MANLY [*saluting Letitia*]. I ought to regard your friends as my own.

CHARLOTTE. Come, Letitia, do give us a little dash of your vivacity; my brother is so sentimental and so grave, that I protest he'll give us the vapours.

MANLY. Though sentiment and gravity, I know, are banished the polite world, yet I hoped they might find some countenance in the meeting of such near connections as brother and sister.

CHARLOTTE. Positively, brother, if you go one step further in this strain, you will set me crying, and that, you know, would spoil my eyes; and then I should never get the husband which our good papa and mamma have so kindly wished me — never be established in the world.

MANLY. Forgive me, my sister, — I am no enemy to mirth ; I love your sprightliness; and I hope it will one day enliven the hours of some worthy man; but when I mention the respectable authors of my existence, — the cherishers and protectors of my helpless infancy, whose hearts glow with such fondness and attachment that they would willingly lay down their lives for my welfare, — you will excuse me if I am so unfashionable as to speak of them with some degree of respect and reverence.

CHARLOTTE. Well, well, brother; if you won t be gay, we'll not differ; I will be as grave as you wish. [*Affects gravity.*] And so, brother, you have come to the city to exchange some of your commutation notes for a little pleasure?

MANLY. Indeed you are mistaken; my errand is not of amusement, but business; and as I neither drink nor game, my expenses will be so trivial, I shall have no occasion to sell my notes.

CHARLOTTE. Then you won t have occasion to do a very good thing. Why, here was the Vermont General — he came down some time since, sold all his musty notes at one stroke, and then laid the cash out in trinkets for his dear Fanny. I want a dozen pretty things myself; have you got the notes with you?

MANLY. I shall be ever willing to contribute, as far as it is in my power, to adorn or in any way to please my sister; yet I hope I shall never be obliged for this to sell my notes. I may be romantic, but I preserve them as a sacred deposit. Their full amount is justly due to me, but as embarrassments, the natural consequences of a long war, disable my country from supporting its credit, I shall wait with patience until it is rich enough to discharge them. If that is not in my day, they shall be transmitted as an honourable certificate to posterity, that I have humbly imitated our illustrious WASHINGTON, in having exposed my health and life in the service of my country, without reaping any other reward than the glory of conquering in so arduous a contest.

CHARLOTTE. Well said heroics. Why, my dear Henry, you have such a lofty way of saying things, that I protest I almost tremble at the thought of introducing you to the polite circles in the city. The belles would think you were a player run mad, with your head filled with old scraps of tragedy; and as to the beaux, they might admire, because they would not understand you. But, however, I must, I believe, introduce you to two or three ladies of my acquaintance.

LETITIA. And that will make him acquainted with thirty or forty beaux.

CHARLOTTE. Oh! brother, you don't know what a fund of happiness you have in store.

MANLY. I fear, sister, I have not refinement sufficient to enjoy it.

CHARLOTTE. Oh! you cannot fail being pleased.

LETITIA. Our ladies are so delicate and dressy.

CHARLOTTE. And our beaux so dressy and delicate.

LETITIA. Our ladies chat and flirt so agreeably.

CHARLOTTE. And our beaux simper and bow so gracefully.

LETITIA. With their hair so trim and neat.

CHARLOTTE. And their faces so soft and sleek.

LETITIA. Their buckles so tonish and bright.

CHARLOTTE. And their hands so slender and white.

LETITIA. I vow, Charlotte, we are quite poetical.

CHARLOTTE. And then, brother, the faces of the beaux are of such a lily-white hue! None of that horrid robustness of constitution, that vulgar cornfed glow of health, which can only serve to alarm an unmarried lady with apprehension, and prove a melancholy memento to a married one, that she can never hope for the happiness of being a widow. I will say this to the credit of our city beaux, that such is the delicacy of their complexion, dress, and address, that, even had I no reliance upon the honour of the dear Adonises, I would trust myself in any possible situation with them, without the least apprehensions of rudeness.

MANLY. Sister Charlotte!

CHARLOTTE. Now, now, now, brother [*interrupting him*], now don't go to spoil my mirth with a dash of your gravity; I am so glad to see you, I am in tip-top spirits. Oh! that you could be with us at a little snug party. There is Billy Simper, Jack Chaffe, and Colonel Van Titter, Miss Promonade, and the two Miss Tambours, sometimes make a party, with some other ladies, in a side-box at the play. Everything is conducted with such decorum. First we bow round to the company in general, then to each one in particular, then we have so many inquiries after each other's health, and we are so happy to meet each other, and it is so many ages since we last had that pleasure, and if a married lady is in company, we have such a sweet dissertation upon her son Bobby's chin-cough; then the curtain rises, then our sensibility is all awake, and then, by the mere force of apprehension, we torture some harmless expression into a double meaning, which the poor author never dreamt of, and then we have recourse to our fans, and then we blush, and then the gentlemen jog one another, peep under the fan, and make the prettiest remarks; and then we giggle and they simper, and they giggle and we simper, and then the curtain drops, and then for nuts and oranges, and then we bow, and it's pray, Ma am, take it, and pray, Sir, keep it, and oh! not for the world, Sir; and then the curtain rises again, and then we blush and giggle and simper and bow all over again. Oh! the sentimental charms of a side-box conversation!     [*All laugh.*

MANLY. Well, sister, I join heartily with you in the laugh; for, in my opinion, it is as justifiable to laugh at folly as it is reprehensible to ridicule misfortune.

CHARLOTTE. Well, but, brother, positively I can't introduce you in these clothes: why, your coat looks as if it were calculated for the vulgar purpose of keeping yourself comfortable.

MANLY. This coat was my regimental coat in the late war. The public tumults of our state have induced me to buckle on the sword in support of that government which I once fought to establish. I can only say, sister, that there was a time when this coat was respectable, and some people even thought that those men who had endured so many winter campaigns in the service of their country, without bread, clothing, or pay, at least deserved that the poverty of their appearance should not be ridiculed.

CHARLOTTE. We agree in opinion entirely, brother, though it would not have done for me to have said it: it is the coat makes the man respectable. In the time of the war, when we were almost fright⁄ened to death, why, your coat was respectable, that is, fashionable; now another kind of coat is fashion⁄able, that is, respectable. And pray direct the taylor to make yours the height of the fashion.

MANLY. Though it is of little consequence to me of what shape my coat is, yet, as to the height of the fashion, there you will please to excuse me, sister. You know my sentiments on that subject. I have of⁄ten lamented the advantage which the French have over us in that particular. In Paris, the fashions have their dawnings, their routine, and declensions, and depend as much upon the caprice of the day as in other countries; but there every lady assumes a right to deviate from the general *ton* as far as will be of advantage to her own appearance. In America, the cry is, what is the fashion? and we follow it indis⁄criminately, because it is so.

CHARLOTTE. Therefore it is, that when large hoops are in fashion, we often see many a plump girl lost in the immensity of a hoop⁄petticoat, whose want of height and *en⁄bon⁄point* would never have been re⁄marked in any other dress. When the high head⁄dress is the mode, how then do we see a lofty cush⁄ion, with a profusion of gauze, feathers, and ribband, supported by a face no bigger than an apple! whilst a broad full-faced lady, who really would have appeared tolerably handsome in a large head-dress, looks with her smart chapeau as masculine as a soldier.

MANLY. But remember, my dear sister, and I wish all my fair country-women would recollect, that the only excuse a young lady can have for going extravagantly into a fashion is because it makes her look extravagantly handsome. — Ladies, I must wish you a good morning.

CHARLOTTE. But, brother, you are going to make home with us.

MANLY. Indeed I cannot. I have seen my uncle and explained that matter.

CHARLOTTE. Come and dine with us, then. We have a family dinner about half-past four o'clock.

MANLY. I am engaged to dine with the Spanish ambassador. I was introduced to him by an old brother officer; and instead of freezing me with a cold card of compliment to dine with him ten days hence, he, with the true old Castilian frankness, in a friendly manner, asked me to dine with him to-day — an honour I could not refuse. Sister, adieu — Madam, your most obedient —— [*Exit.*

CHARLOTTE. I will wait upon you to the door, brother; I have something particular to say to you.

[*Exit.*

LETITIA [*alone*]. What a pair! —She the pink of flirtation, he the essence of everything that is *outre* and gloomy. — I think I have completely deceived Charlotte by my manner of speaking of Mr. Dimple; she's too much the friend of Maria to be confided in. He is certainly rendering himself disagreeable to Maria, in order to break with her and proffer his hand to me. This is what the delicate fellow hinted in our last conversation.                    [*Exit.*

## SCENE II. *The Mall*

### *Enter* JESSAMY

JESSAMY. Positively this Mall is a very pretty place. I hope the cits won t ruin it by repairs. To be sure, it won't do to speak of in the same day with Ranelegh or Vauxhall; however, it's a fine place for a young fel- low to display his person to advantage. Indeed, noth- ing is lost here; the girls have taste, and I am very happy to find they have adopted the elegant London fashion of looking back, after a genteel fellow like me has passed them. — Ah! who comes here? This, by his awkwardness, must be the Yankee colonel's servant. I'll accost him.

### *Enter* JONATHAN

Votre tres-humble serviteur, Monsieur. I under- stand Colonel Manly, the Yankee officer, has the hon- our of your services.

JONATHAN. Sir !——

JESSAMY. I say, Sir, I understand that Colonel Manly has the honour of having you for a servant.

JONATHAN. Servant! Sir, do you take me for a neger,—I am Colonel Manly's waiter.

JESSAMY. A true Yankee distinction, egad, without a difference. Why, Sir, do you not perform all the offices of a servant? do you not even blacken his boots?

JONATHAN. Yes; I do grease them a bit sometimes; but I am a true blue son of liberty, for all that. Father said I should come as Colonel Manly's waiter, to see the world, and all that; but no man shall master me. My father has as good a farm as the colonel.

JESSAMY. Well, Sir, we will not quarrel about terms upon the eve of an acquaintance from which I promise myself so much satisfaction; — therefore, sans ceremonie——

JONATHAN. What?——

JESSAMY. I say I am extremely happy to see Colonel Manly's waiter.

JONATHAN. Well, and I vow, too, I am pretty considerably glad to see you; but what the dogs need of all this outlandish lingo? Who may you be, Sir, if I may be so bold?

JESSAMY. I have the honour to be Mr. Dimple's servant, or, if you please, waiter. We lodge under the same roof, and should be glad of the honour of your acquaintance.

JONATHAN. You a waiter! by the living jingo, you look so topping, I took you for one of the agents to Congress.

JESSAMY. The brute has discernment, notwith standing his appearance.—Give me leave to say I wonder then at your familiarity.

JONATHAN. Why, as to the matter of that, Mr. ——; pray, what's your name?

JESSAMY. Jessamy, at your service.

JONATHAN. Why, I swear we don't make any great matter of distinction in our state between quality and other folks.

JESSAMY. This is, indeed, a levelling principle. — I hope, Mr. Jonathan, you have not taken part with the insurgents.

JONATHAN. Why, since General Shays has sneaked off and given us the bag to hold, I don't care to give my opinion; but you'll promise not to tell — put your ear this way — you won't tell? — I vow I did think the sturgeons were right.

JESSAMY. I thought, Mr. Jonathan, you Massa chusetts men always argued with a gun in your hand. Why didn't you join them?

JONATHAN. Why, the colonel is one of those folks called the Shin — Shin — dang it all, I can't speak them lignum vitæ words — you know who I mean — there is a company of them — they wear a china goose at their button-hole — a kind of gilt thing. — Now the colonel told father and brother, — you must know there are, let me see — there is Elnathan, Silas, and Barnabas, Tabitha — no, no, she's a she — tarnation, now I have it — there's Elnathan, Silas, Barnabas, Jonathan, that's I — seven of us, six went into the wars, and I staid at home to take care of mother. Colonel said that it was a burning shame for the true blue Bunker Hill sons of liberty, who had fought Governor Hutchinson, Lord North, and the Devil, to have any hand in kicking up a cursed dust against a government which we had, every mother's son of us, a hand in making.

JESSAMY. Bravo! — Well, have you been abroad in the city since your arrival? What have you seen that is curious and entertaining?

JONATHAN. Oh! I have seen a power of fine sights. I went to see two marble-stone men and a leaden horse that stands out in doors in all weathers; and when I came where they was, one had got no head, and t'other wern't there. They said as how the leaden man was a damn'd tory, and that he took wit in his anger and rode off in the time of the troubles.

JESSAMY. But this was not the end of your excursion?

JONATHAN. Oh, no; I went to a place they call Holy Ground. Now I counted this was a place where folks go to meeting; so I put my hymn-book in my pocket, and walked softly and grave as a minister; and when I came there, the dogs a bit of a meeting-house could I see. At last I spied a young gentle-woman standing by one of the seats which they have here at the doors. I took her to be the deacon's daugh-ter, and she looked so kind, and so obliging, that I thought I would go and ask her the way to lecture, and — would you think it? — she called me dear, and sweeting, and honey, just as if we were married: by the living jingo, I had a month's mind to buss her.

JESSAMY. Well, but how did it end?

JONATHAN. Why, as I was standing talking with her, a parcel of sailor men and boys got round me, the snarl-headed curs fell a-kicking and cursing of me at such a tarnal rate, that I vow I was glad to take to my heels and split home, right off, tail on end, like a stream of chalk.

JESSAMY. Why, my dear friend, you are not ac-quainted with the city; that girl you saw was a——— *[Whispers.*

JONATHAN. Mercy on my soul! was that young woman a harlot! — Well! if this is New-York Holy Ground, what must the Holy-day Ground be!

JESSAMY. Well, you should not judge of the city

too rashly. We have a number of elegant, fine girls here that make a man's leisure hours pass very agree, ably. I would esteem it an honour to announce you to some of them. — Gad! that announce is a select word; I wonder where I picked it up.

JONATHAN. I don't want to know them.

JESSAMY. Come, come, my dear friend, I see that I must assume the honour of being the director of your amusements. Nature has given us passions, and youth and opportunity stimulate to gratify them. It is no shame, my dear Blueskin, for a man to amuse himself with a little gallantry.

JONATHAN. Girl huntry! I don't altogether under, stand. I never played at that game. I know how to play hunt the squirrel, but I can't play anything with the girls; I am as good as married.

JESSAMY. Vulgar, horrid brute! Married, and above a hundred miles from his wife, and thinks that an ob, jection to his making love to every woman he meets! He never can have read, no, he never can have been in a room with a volume of the divine Chesterfield. — So you are married?

JONATHAN. No, I don't say so; I said I was as good as married, a kind of promise.

JESSAMY. As good as married! ——

JONATHAN. Why, yes; there's Tabitha Wymen, the deacon's daughter, at home; she and I have been courting a great while, and folks say as how we are to be married; and so I broke a piece of money with her when we parted, and she promised not to spark it with Solomon Dyer while I am gone. You wou'dn't have me false to my true-love, would you?

JESSAMY. May be you have another reason for constancy; possibly the young lady has a fortune? Ha! Mr. Jonathan, the solid charms: the chains of love are never so binding as when the links are made of gold.

JONATHAN. Why, as to fortune, I must needs say her father is pretty dumb rich; he went representa-tive for our town last year. He will give her—let me see —four times seven is—seven times four— nought and carry one, — he will give her twenty acres of land— somewhat rocky though—a Bible, and a cow.

JESSAMY. Twenty acres of rock, a Bible, and a cow! Why, my dear Mr. Jonathan, we have servant-maids, or, as you would more elegantly express it, waitresses, in this city, who collect more in one year from their mistresses' cast clothes.

JONATHAN. You don't say so!——

JESSAMY. Yes, and I'll introduce you to one of them. There is a little lump of flesh and delicacy that lives at next door, waitress to Miss Maria; we often see her on the stoop.

JONATHAN. But are you sure she would be courted by me?

JESSAMY. Never doubt it; remember a faint heart never— blisters on my tongue—I was going to be guilty of a vile proverb; flat against the authority of Chesterfield. I say there can be no doubt that the brilliancy of your merit will secure you a favourable reception.

JONATHAN. Well, but what must I say to her?

JESSAMY. Say to her! why, my dear friend, though I admire your profound knowledge on every other subject, yet, you will pardon my saying that your want of opportunity has made the female heart escape the poignancy of your penetration. Say to her! Why, when a man goes a-courting, and hopes for success, he must begin with doing, and not saying.

JONATHAN. Well, what must I do?

JESSAMY. Why, when you are introduced you must make five or six elegant bows.

JONATHAN. Six elegant bows! I understand that; six, you say? Well——

JESSAMY. Then you must press and kiss her hand; then press and kiss, and so on to her lips and cheeks; then talk as much as you can about hearts, darts, flames, nectar and ambrosia — the more incoherent the better.

JONATHAN. Well, but suppose she should be angry with I?

JESSAMY. Why, if she should pretend—please to observe, Mr. Jonathan—if she should pretend to be offended, you must——But I'll tell you how my master acted in such a case: He was seated by a young lady of eighteen upon a sofa, plucking with a wanton hand the blooming sweets of youth and beauty. When the lady thought it necessary to check his ardour, she called up a frown upon her lovely face, so irresistibly alluring, that it would have warmed the frozen bosom of age; remember, said she, putting her delicate arm upon his, remember your character and my honour. My master instantly dropped upon his knees, with eyes swimming with love, cheeks glowing with desire, and in the gentlest modulation of voice he said: My dear Caroline, in a few months our hands will be indissolubly united at the altar; our hearts I feel are already so; the favours you now grant as evidence of your affection are favours indeed; yet, when the ceremony is once past, what will now be received with rapture will then be attributed to duty.

JONATHAN. Well, and what was the consequence?

JESSAMY. The consequence!—Ah! forgive me, my dear friend, but you New England gentlemen have such a laudable curiosity of seeing the bottom of everything;—why, to be honest, I confess I saw the blooming cherub of a consequence smiling in its angelic mother's arms, about ten months afterwards.

JONATHAN. Well, if I follow all your plans, make them six bows, and all that, shall I have such little cherubim consequences?

JESSAMY. Undoubtedly. — What are you musing upon?

JONATHAN. You say you'll certainly make me ac-quainted? — Why, I was thinking then how I should contrive to pass this broken piece of silver — won't it buy a sugar-dram?

JESSAMY. What is that, the love-token from the deacon's daughter? — You come on bravely. But I must hasten to my master. Adieu, my dear friend.

JONATHAN. Stay, Mr. Jessamy — must I buss her when I am introduced to her?

JESSAMY. I told you, you must kiss her.

JONATHAN. Well, but must I buss her?

JESSAMY. Why kiss and buss, and buss and kiss, is all one.

JONATHAN. Oh! my dear friend, though you have a profound knowledge of all, a pugnency of tribula-tion, you don't know everything. [*Exit.*

JESSAMY [*alone*]. Well, certainly I improve; my master could not have insinuated himself with more address into the heart of a man he despised. Now will this blundering dog sicken Jenny with his nauseous pawings, until she flies into my arms for very ease. How sweet will the contrast be between the blundering Jonathan and the courtly and accomplished Jessamy!

*he said the thing!*

END OF THE SECOND ACT

## ACT III. SCENE I

### DIMPLE'S *Room*

#### DIMPLE *discovered at a Toilet*

DIMPLE [*reading*]: "Women have in general but one object, which is their beauty." Very true, my lord; positively very true. "Nature has hardly formed a woman ugly enough to be insensible to flattery upon her person." Extremely just, my lord; every day's delightful experience confirms this. "If her face is so shocking that she must, in some degree, be conscious of it, her figure and air, she thinks, make ample amends for it." The sallow Miss Wan is a proof of this. Upon my telling the distasteful wretch, the other day, that her countenance spoke the pensive language of sentiment, and that Lady Wortley Montagu declared that if the ladies were arrayed in the garb of innocence, the face would be the last part which would be admired, as Monsieur Milton expresses it, she grinn'd horribly a ghastly smile. "If her figure is deformed, she thinks her face counterbalances it."

*Enter* JESSAMY *with letters*

Where got you these, Jessamy?

JESSAMY. Sir, the English packet is arrived.

DIMPLE [*opens and reads a letter enclosing notes*]:

"Sir,

"I have drawn bills on you in favour of Messrs.
Van Cash and Co. as per margin. I have taken up
your note to Col. Piquet, and discharged your debts
to my Lord Lurcher and Sir Harry Rook. I herewith
enclose you copies of the bills, which I have no doubt
will be immediately honoured. On failure, I shall em-
power some lawyer in your country to recover the
amounts.

"I am, Sir,

"Your most humble servant,

"JOHN HAZARD."

Now, did not my lord expressly say that it was unbecoming a well-bred man to be in a passion, I confess I should be ruffled. [*Reads.*] "There is no accident so unfortunate, which a wise man may not turn
to his advantage; nor any accident so fortunate, which
a fool will not turn to his disadvantage." True, my
lord; but how advantage can be derived from this I
can't see. Chesterfield himself, who made, however,
the worst practice of the most excellent precepts, was
never in so embarrassing a situation. I love the person of Charlotte, and it is necessary I should command the fortune of Letitia. As to Maria!—I doubt
not by my *sang-froid* behaviour I shall compel her to

decline the match; but the blame must not fall upon me. A prudent man, as my lord says, should take all the credit of a good action to himself, and throw the discredit of a bad one upon others. I must break with Maria, marry Letitia, and as for Charlotte—why, Charlotte must be a companion to my wife.—Here, Jessamy!

*Enter* JESSAMY

DIMPLE *folds and seals two letters*

DIMPLE. Here, Jessamy, take this letter to my love.

[*Gives one.*

JESSAMY. To which of your honour's loves?— Oh! [*reading*] to Miss Letitia, your honour's rich love.

DIMPLE. And this [*delivers another*] to Miss Char⸗ lotte Manly. See that you deliver them privately.

JESSAMY. Yes, your honour. [*Going.*

DIMPLE. Jessamy, who are these strange lodgers that came to the house last night?

JESSAMY. Why, the master is a Yankee colonel; I have not seen much of him; but the man is the most unpolished animal your honour ever disgraced your eyes by looking upon. I have had one of the most *outre* conversations with him!—He really has a most prodigious effect upon my risibility.

DIMPLE. I ought, according to every rule of Ches⸗

terfield, to wait on him and insinuate myself into his good graces.——Jessamy, wait on the colonel with my compliments, and if he is disengaged I will do my‑self the honour of paying him my respects.—Some ignorant, unpolished boor ——

JESSAMY *goes off and returns*

JESSAMY. Sir, the colonel is gone out, and Jona‑than his servant says that he is gone to stretch his legs upon the Mall.—Stretch his legs! what an indelicacy of diction!

DIMPLE. Very well. Reach me my hat and sword. I'll accost him there, in my way to Letitia's, as by accident; pretend to be struck by his person and address, and endeavour to steal into his confidence. Jessamy, I have no business for you at present. [*Exit.*

JESSAMY [*taking up the book*]. My master and I ob‑tain our knowledge from the same source;—though, gad! I think myself much the prettier fellow of the two. [*Surveying himself in the glass.*] That was a bril‑liant thought, to insinuate that I folded my master's letters for him; the folding is so neat, that it does hon‑our to the operator. I once intended to have insinu‑ated that I wrote his letters too; but that was before I saw them; it won t do now; no honour there, posi‑tively.—"Nothing looks more vulgar, [*reading af‑fectedly*] ordinary, and illiberal than ugly, uneven, and ragged nails; the ends of which should be kept even and clean, not tipped with black, and cut in small segments of circles."—Segments of circles! surely my lord did not consider that he wrote for the beaux. Segments of circles; what a crabbed term! Now I dare answer that my master, with all his learning, does not know that this means, according to the present mode, let the nails grow long, and then cut them off even at top. [*Laughing without.*] Ha! that's Jenny's titter. I protest I despair of ever teaching that girl to laugh; she has something so execrably natural in her laugh, that I declare it absolutely discomposes my nerves. How came she into our House! [*Calls.*] Jenny!

### *Enter* JENNY

Prythee, Jenny, don't spoil your fine face with laughing.

JENNY. Why, mustn't I laugh, Mr. Jessamy?

JESSAMY. You may smile, but, as my lord says, nothing can authorise a laugh.

JENNY. Well, but I can't help laughing.—Have you seen him, Mr. Jessamy? ha, ha, ha!

JESSAMY. Seen whom?

JENNY. Why, Jonathan, the New England colo nel's servant. Do you know he was at the play last night, and the stupid creature don't know where he has been. He would not go to a play for the world; he thinks it was a show, as he calls it.

JESSAMY. As ignorant and unpolished as he is, do you know, Miss Jenny, that I propose to introduce him to the honour of your acquaintance?

JENNY. Introduce him to me! for what?

JESSAMY. Why, my lovely girl, that you may take him under your protection, as Madame Rambouillet did young Stanhope; that you may, by your plastic hand, mould this uncouth cub into a gentleman. He is to make love to you.

JENNY. Make love to me! ——

JESSAMY. Yes, Mistress Jenny, make love to you; and, I doubt not, when he shall become *domesticated* in your kitchen, that this boor, under your auspices, will soon become *un amiable petit Jonathan.*

JENNY. I must say, Mr. Jessamy, if he copies after me, he will be vastly, monstrously polite.

JESSAMY. Stay here one moment, and I will call him. — Jonathan! — Mr. Jonathan! —  [*Calls.*

JONATHAN [*within*]. Holla! there. — [*Enters.*] You promise to stand by me — six bows you say.  [*Bows.*

JESSAMY. Mrs. Jenny, I have the honour of pre´ senting Mr. Jonathan, Colonel Manly's waiter, to you. I am extremely happy that I have it in my power to make two worthy people acquainted with each other's merits.

JENNY. So, Mr. Jonathan, I hear you were at the play last night.

JONATHAN. At the play! why, did you think I went to the devil's drawing-room?

JENNY. The devil's drawing-room!

JONATHAN. Yes; why an't cards and dice the devil's device, and the play-house the shop where the devil hangs out the vanities of the world upon the tenter-hooks of temptation? I believe you have not heard how they were acting the old boy one night, and the wicked one came among them sure enough, and went right off in a storm, and carried one quarter of the play-house with him. Oh! no, no, no! you won t catch me at a play-house, I warrant you.

JENNY. Well, Mr. Jonathan, though I don't scruple your veracity, I have some reasons for believing you were there: pray, where were you about six o'clock?

JONATHAN. Why, I went to see one Mr. Morrison, the *hocus pocus* man; they said as how he could eat a case knife.

JENNY. Well, and how did you find the place?

JONATHAN. As I was going about here and there, to and again, to find it, I saw a great crowd of folks going into a long entry that had lantherns over the door; so I asked a man whether that was not the place where they played *hocus pocus?* He was a very civil, kind man, though he did speak like the Hessians; he lifted up his eyes and said, "They play *hocus pocus* tricks enough there, Got knows, mine friend."

JENNY. Well—

JONATHAN. So I went right in, and they shewed me away, clean up to the garret, just like meeting/house gallery. And so I saw a power of topping folks, all sitting round in little cabbins, "just like father's corn/cribs"; and then there was such a squeaking with the fiddles, and such a tarnal blaze with the lights, my head was near turned. At last the people that sat near me set up such a hissing—hiss—like so many mad cats; and then they went thump, thump, thump, just like our Peleg threshing wheat, and stampt away, just like the nation; and called out for one Mr. Langolee,—I suppose he helps act the tricks.

JENNY. Well, and what did you do all this time?

JONATHAN. Gor, I—I liked the fun, and so I thumpt away, and hiss'd as lustily as the best of 'em. One sailor/looking man that sat by me, seeing me stamp, and knowing I was a cute fellow, because I could make a roaring noise, clapt me on the shoulder and said, "You are a d    d hearty cock, smite my timbers!" I told him so I was, but I thought he need not swear so, and make use of such naughty words.

JESSAMY. The savage!—Well, and did you see the man with his tricks?

JONATHAN. Why, I vow, as I was looking out for him, they lifted up a great green cloth and let us look right into the next neighbour's house. Have you a good many houses in New-York made so in that 'ere way?

JENNY. Not many; but did you see the family?

JONATHAN. Yes, swamp it; I see'd the family.

JENNY. Well, and how did you like them?

JONATHAN. Why, I vow they were pretty much like other families;—there was a poor, good-natured, curse of a husband, and a sad rantipole of a wife.

JENNY. But did you see no other folks?

JONATHAN. Yes. There was one youngster; they called him Mr. Joseph; he talked as sober and as pious as a minister; but, like some ministers that I know, he was a sly tike in his heart for all that. He was going to ask a young woman to spark it with him, and—the Lord have mercy on my soul!—she was another man's wife.

JESSAMY. The Wabash!

JENNY. And did you see any more folks?

JONATHAN. Why, they came on as thick as mus-tard. For my part, I thought the house was haunted. There was a soldier fellow, who talked about his row de dow, dow, and courted a young woman; but, of all the cute folk I saw, I liked one little fellow ——

JENNY. Aye! who was he?

JONATHAN. Why, he had red hair, and a little round plump face like mine, only not altogether so handsome. His name was—Darby;—that was his baptizing name; his other name I forgot. Oh! it was Wig—Wag—Wag'all, Darby Wag'all,—pray, do you know him?—I should like to take a sling with him, or a drap of cyder with a pepper'pod in it, to make it warm and comfortable.

JENNY. I can't say I have that pleasure.

JONATHAN. I wish you did; he is a cute fellow. But there was one thing I didn't like in that Mr. Darby; and that was, he was afraid of some of them 'ere shooting irons, such as your troopers wear on training days. Now, I'm a true born Yankee American son of liberty, and I never was afraid of a gun yet in all my life.

JENNY. Well, Mr. Jonathan, you were certainly at the play'house.

JONATHAN. I at the play'house!—Why didn't I see the play then?

JENNY. Why, the people you saw were players.

JONATHAN. Mercy on my soul! did I see the wicked players?—Mayhap that 'ere Darby that I liked so was the old serpent himself, and had his clo'ven foot in his pocket. Why, I vow, now I come to think on't, the candles seemed to burn blue, and I am sure where I sat it smelt tarnally of brimstone.

JESSAMY. Well, Mr. Jonathan, from your account, which I confess is very accurate, you must have been at the play-house.

JONATHAN. Why, I vow, I began to smell a rat. When I came away, I went to the man for my money again; you want your money? says he; yes, says I; for what? says he; why, says I, no man shall jocky me out of my money; I paid my money to see sights, and the dogs a bit of a sight have I seen, unless you call listening to people's private business a sight. Why, says he, it is the School for Scandalization. — The School for Scandalization! — Oh! ho! no wonder you New-York folks are so cute at it, when you go to school to learn it; and so I jogged off.

JESSAMY. My dear Jenny, my master's business drags me from you; would to heaven I knew no other servitude than to your charms.

JONATHAN. Well, but don't go; you won't leave me so———

JESSAMY. Excuse me. — Remember the cash.

[*Aside to him, and — Exit.*

JENNY. Mr. Jonathan, won't you please to sit down? Mr. Jessamy tells me you wanted to have some con-versation with me.

[*Having brought forward two chairs, they sit.*

JONATHAN. Ma'am!———

JENNY. Sir!———

JONATHAN. Ma'am!——

JENNY. Pray, how do you like the city, Sir?

JONATHAN. Ma'am!——

JENNY. I say, Sir, how do you like New-York?

JONATHAN. Ma am!——

JENNY. The stupid creature! but I must pass some little time with him, if it is only to endeavour to learn whether it was his master that made such an abrupt entrance into our house, and my young mistress's heart, this morning. [*Aside*.] As you don't seem to like to talk, Mr. Jonathan — do you sing?

JONATHAN. Gor, I — I am glad she asked that, for I forgot what Mr. Jessamy bid me say, and I dare as well be hanged as act what he bid me do, I'm so ashamed. [*Aside*.] Yes, Ma'am, I can sing — I can sing Mear, Old Hundred, and Bangor.

JENNY. Oh! I don't mean psalm tunes. Have you no little song to please the ladies, such as Roslin Castle, or the Maid of the Mill?

JONATHAN. Why, all my tunes go to meeting tunes, save one, and I count you won't altogether like that 'ere.

JENNY. What is it called?

JONATHAN. I am sure you have heard folks talk about it; it is called Yankee Doodle.

JENNY. Oh! it is the tune I am fond of; and if I know anything of my mistress, she would be glad to dance to it. Pray, sing!

JONATHAN [*sings*].

> Father and I went up to camp,
> Along with Captain Goodwin ;
> And there we saw the men and boys,
> As thick as hasty-pudding.
>
>> Yankee doodle do, etc.

> And there we saw a swamping gun,
> Big as log of maple,
> On a little deuced cart,
> A load for father's cattle.
>
>> Yankee doodle do, etc.

> And every time they fired it off
> It took a horn of powder,
> It made a noise — like father's gun,
> Only a nation louder.
>
>> Yankee doodle do, etc.

> There was a man in our town,
> His name was ——

No, no, that won't do. Now, if I was with Tabitha Wymen and Jemima Cawley down at father Chase's, I shouldn't mind singing this all out before them— you would be affronted if I was to sing that, though that's a lucky thought ; if you should be affronted, I have something dang'd cute, which Jessamy told me to say to you.

JENNY. Is that all ! I assure you I like it of all things.

JONATHAN. No, no ; I can sing more ; some other time, when you and I are better acquainted, I'll sing

the whole of it — no, no — that's a fib — I can t sing
but a hundred and ninety verses; our Tabitha at home
can sing it all. —— *[Sings.*

> Marblehead's a rocky place,
> And Cape-Cod is sandy;
> Charlestown is burnt down,
> Boston is the dandy.
>> Yankee doodle, doodle do, etc.

I vow, my own town song has put me into such topping spirits that I believe I'll begin to do a little, as
Jessamy says we must when we go a-courting —
[*Runs and kisses her.*] Burning rivers! cooling
flames! red-hot roses! pig-nuts! hasty-pudding and
ambrosia!

JENNY. What means this freedom? you insulting
wretch. *[Strikes him.*

JONATHAN. Are you affronted?

JENNY. Affronted! with what looks shall I express
my anger?

JONATHAN. Looks! why as to the matter of looks,
you look as cross as a witch.

JENNY. Have you no feeling for the delicacy of
my sex?

JONATHAN. Feeling! Gor, I — I feel the delicacy
of your sex pretty smartly [*rubbing his cheek*], though,
I vow, I thought when you city ladies courted and
married, and all that, you put feeling out of the ques-

tion. But I want to know whether you are really affronted, or only pretend to be so? 'Cause, if you are certainly right down affronted, I am at the end of my tether; Jessamy didn't tell me what to say to you.

JENNY. Pretend to be affronted!

JONATHAN. Aye aye, if you only pretend, you shall hear how I'll go to work to make cherubim consequences.                               [Runs up to her.

JENNY. Begone, you brute!

JONATHAN. That looks like mad; but I won't lose my speech. My dearest Jenny — your name is Jenny, I think? — My dearest Jenny, though I have the highest esteem for the sweet favours you have just now granted me — Gor, that's a fib, though; but Jessamy says it is not wicked to tell lies to the women. [Aside.] I say, though I have the highest esteem for the favours you have just now granted me, yet you will consider that, as soon as the dissolvable knot is tied, they will no longer be favours, but only matters of duty and matters of course.

JENNY. Marry you! you audacious monster! get out of my sight, or, rather, let me fly from you.

[Exit hastily.

JONATHAN. Gor! she's gone off in a swinging passion, before I had time to think of consequences. If this is the way with your city ladies, give me the twenty acres of rock, the Bible, the cow, and Tabitha, and a little peaceable bundling.

## SCENE II. *The Mall*

### *Enter* MANLY

MANLY. It must be so, Montague! and it is not all the tribe of Mandevilles that shall convince me that a nation, to become great, must first become dissi‐pated. Luxury is surely the bane of a nation: Luxury! which enervates both soul and body, by opening a thousand new sources of enjoyment, opens, also, a thousand new sources of contention and want: Lux‐ury! which renders a people weak at home, and ac‐cessible to bribery, corruption, and force from abroad. When the Grecian states knew no other tools than the axe and the saw, the Grecians were a great, a free, and a happy people. The kings of Greece devoted their lives to the service of their country, and her sen‐ators knew no other superiority over their fellow‐citizens than a glorious pre‐eminence in danger and virtue. They exhibited to the world a noble spectacle, —a number of independent states united by a simi‐larity of language, sentiment, manners, common in‐terest, and common consent in one grand mutual league of protection. And, thus united, long might they have continued the cherishers of arts and sci‐ences, the protectors of the oppressed, the scourge of tyrants, and the safe asylum of liberty. But when for‐eign gold, and still more pernicious foreign luxury, had crept among them, they sapped the vitals of their virtue. The virtues of their ancestors were only found in their writings. Envy and suspicion, the vices of little minds, possessed them. The various states engendered jealousies of each other; and, more unfortunately, growing jealous of their great federal council, the Amphictyons, they forgot that their common safety had existed, and would exist, in giving them an honourable extensive prerogative. The common good was lost in the pursuit of private interest; and that people who, by uniting, might have stood against the world in arms, by dividing, crumbled into ruin; — their name is now only known in the page of the historian, and what they once were is all we have left to admire. Oh! that America! Oh! that my country, would, in this her day, learn the things which belong to her peace!

*Enter* DIMPLE

DIMPLE. You are Colonel Manly, I presume?

MANLY. At your service, Sir.

DIMPLE. My name is Dimple, Sir. I have the honour to be a lodger in the same house with you, and, hearing you were in the Mall, came hither to take the liberty of joining you.

MANLY. You are very obliging, Sir.

DIMPLE. As I understand you are a stranger here,

Sir, I have taken the liberty to introduce myself to your acquaintance, as possibly I may have it in my power to point out some things in this city worthy your notice.

MANLY. An attention to strangers is worthy a liberal mind, and must ever be gratefully received. But to a soldier, who has no fixed abode, such atten/ tions are particularly pleasing.

DIMPLE. Sir, there is no character so respectable as that of a soldier. And, indeed, when we reflect how much we owe to those brave men who have suffered so much in the service of their country, and secured to us those inestimable blessings that we now enjoy, our liberty and independence, they demand every attention which gratitude can pay. For my own part, I never meet an officer, but I embrace him as my friend, nor a private in distress, but I insen/ sibly extend my charity to him.——I have hit the Bumkin off very tolerably. [*Aside.*

MANLY. Give me your hand, Sir! I do not proffer this hand to everybody; but you steal into my heart. I hope I am as insensible to flattery as most men; but I declare (it may be my weak side) that I never hear the name of soldier mentioned with respect, but I ex/ perience a thrill of pleasure which I never feel on any other occasion.

DIMPLE. Will you give me leave, my dear Colonel,

to confer an obligation on myself, by shewing you some civilities during your stay here, and giving a similar opportunity to some of my friends?

MANLY. Sir, I thank you; but I believe my stay in this city will be very short.

DIMPLE. I can introduce you to some men of excel⁄lent sense, in whose company you will esteem your⁄self happy; and, by way of amusement, to some fine girls, who will listen to your soft things with pleasure.

MANLY. Sir, I should be proud of the honour of being acquainted with those gentlemen; — but, as for the ladies, I don't understand you.

DIMPLE. Why, Sir, I need not tell you, that when a young gentleman is alone with a young lady he must say some soft things to her fair cheek — indeed, the lady will expect it. To be sure, there is not much pleasure when a man of the world and a finished co⁄quette meet, who perfectly know each other; but how delicious is it to excite the emotions of joy, hope, expectation, and delight in the bosom of a lovely girl who believes every tittle of what you say to be serious!

MANLY. Serious, Sir! In my opinion, the man who, under pretensions of marriage, can plant thorns in the bosom of an innocent, unsuspecting girl is more detestable than a common robber, in the same pro⁄portion as private violence is more despicable than open force, and money of less value than happiness.

DIMPLE. How he awes me by the superiority of his sentiments. [*Aside*.] As you say, Sir, a gentle-man should be cautious how he mentions marriage.

MANLY. Cautious, Sir! No person more approves of an intercourse between the sexes than I do. Fe-male conversation softens our manners, whilst our discourse, from the superiority of our literary advan-tages, improves their minds. But, in our young coun-try, where there is no such thing as gallantry, when a gentleman speaks of love to a lady, whether he men-tions marriage or not, she ought to conclude either that he meant to insult her or that his intentions are the most serious and honourable. How mean, how cruel, is it, by a thousand tender assiduities, to win the affections of an amiable girl, and, though you leave her virtue unspotted, to betray her into the ap-pearance of so many tender partialities, that every man of delicacy would suppress his inclination to-wards her, by supposing her heart engaged! Can any man, for the trivial gratification of his leisure hours, affect the happiness of a whole life! His not having spoken of marriage may add to his perfidy, but can be no excuse for his conduct.

DIMPLE. Sir, I admire your sentiments;—they are mine. The light observations that fell from me were only a principle of the tongue; they came not from the heart; my practice has ever disapproved these principles.

MANLY. I believe you, sir. I should with reluc⁄
tance suppose that those pernicious sentiments could
find admittance into the heart of a gentleman.

DIMPLE. I am now, Sir, going to visit a family,
where, if you please, I will have the honour of in⁄
troducing you. Mr. Manly's ward, Miss Letitia, is a
young lady of immense fortune; and his niece, Miss
Charlotte Manly, is a young lady of great sprightli⁄
ness and beauty.

MANLY. That gentleman, Sir, is my uncle, and
Miss Manly my sister.

DIMPLE. The devil she is! [*Aside.*] Miss Manly
your sister, Sir? I rejoice to hear it, and feel a double
pleasure in being known to you.——Plague on him!
I wish he was at Boston again, with all my soul.

[*Aside.*

MANLY. Come, Sir, will you go?

DIMPLE. I will follow you in a moment, Sir. [*Exit*
MANLY.] Plague on it! this is unlucky. A fighting
brother is a cursed appendage to a fine girl. Egad! I
just stopped in time; had he not discovered himself,
in two minutes more I should have told him how well
I was with his sister. Indeed, I cannot see the satis⁄
faction of an intrigue, if one can t have the pleasure
of communicating it to our friends.          [*Exit.*

END OF THE THIRD ACT

## ACT IV. SCENE I

CHARLOTTE'S *Apartment*

CHARLOTTE *leading in* MARIA

CHARLOTTE. This is so kind, my sweet friend, to come to see me at this moment. I declare, if I were going to be married in a few days, as you are, I should scarce have found time to visit my friends.

MARIA. Do you think, then, that there is an impropriety in it?—How should you dispose of your time?

CHARLOTTE. Why, I should be shut up in my chamber; and my head would so run upon—upon—upon the solemn ceremony that I was to pass through!—I declare, it would take me above two hours merely to learn that little monosyllable—*Yes.* Ah! my dear, your sentimental imagination does not conceive what that little tiny word implies.

MARIA. Spare me your raillery, my sweet friend; I should love your agreeable vivacity at any other time.

CHARLOTTE. Why, this is the very time to amuse you. You grieve me to see you look so unhappy.

MARIA. Have I not reason to look so?

CHARLOTTE. What new grief distresses you?

MARIA. Oh! how sweet it is, when the heart is

borne down with misfortune, to recline and repose on the bosom of friendship! Heaven knows that, although it is improper for a young lady to praise a gentleman, yet I have ever concealed Mr. Dimple's foibles, and spoke of him as of one whose reputation I expected would be linked with mine; but his late conduct towards me has turned my coolness into contempt. He behaves as if he meant to insult and disgust me; whilst my father, in the last conversation on the subject of our marriage, spoke of it as a matter which lay near his heart, and in which he would not bear contradiction.

CHARLOTTE. This works well; oh! the generous Dimple. I'll endeavour to excite her to discharge him. [*Aside.*] But, my dear friend, your happiness depends on yourself. Why don't you discard him? Though the match has been of long standing, I would not be forced to make myself miserable: no parent in the world should oblige me to marry the man I did not like.

MARIA. Oh! my dear, you never lived with your parents, and do not know what influence a father's frowns have upon a daughter's heart. Besides, what have I to alledge against Mr. Dimple, to justify myself to the world? He carries himself so smoothly, that every one would impute the blame to me, and call me capricious.

CHARLOTTE. And call her capricious! Did ever such an objection start into the heart of woman? For my part, I wish I had fifty lovers to discard, for no other reason than because I did not fancy them. My dear Maria, you will forgive me; I know your candour and confidence in me; but I have at times, I confess, been led to suppose that some other gentleman was the cause of your aversion to Mr. Dimple.

MARIA. No, my sweet friend, you may be assured, that though I have seen many gentlemen I could prefer to Mr. Dimple, yet I never saw one that I thought I could give my hand to, until this morning.

CHARLOTTE. This morning!

MARIA. Yes; one of the strangest accidents in the world. The odious Dimple, after disgusting me with his conversation, had just left me, when a gentleman, who, it seems, boards in the same house with him, saw him coming out of our door, and, the houses looking very much alike, he came into our house instead of his lodgings; nor did he discover his mistake until he got into the parlour, where I was; he then bowed so gracefully, made such a genteel apology, and looked so manly and noble! ——

CHARLOTTE. I see some folks, though it is so great an impropriety, can praise a gentleman, when he happens to be the man of their fancy.          [*Aside.*

MARIA. I don't know how it was, — I hope he did

not think me indelicate, — but I asked him, I believe, to sit down, or pointed to a chair. He sat down,
and, instead of having recourse to observations upon
the weather, or hackneyed criticisms upon the theatre, he entered readily into a conversation worthy a
man of sense to speak, and a lady of delicacy and sentiment to hear. He was not strictly handsome, but he
spoke the language of sentiment, and his eyes looked
tenderness and honour.

CHARLOTTE. Oh! [*eagerly*] you sentimental, grave
girls, when your hearts are once touched, beat us rattles
a bar's length. And so you are quite in love with this
he-angel?

MARIA. In love with him! How can you rattle so,
Charlotte? am I not going to be miserable? [*Sighs.*]
In love with a gentleman I never saw but one hour in
my life, and don t know his name! No; I only wished
that the man I shall marry may look, and talk, and
act, just like him. Besides, my dear, he is a married
man.

CHARLOTTE. Why, that was good-natured — he
told you so, I suppose, in mere charity, to prevent you
falling in love with him?

MARIA. He didn't tell me so; [*peevishly*] he looked
as if he was married.

CHARLOTTE. How, my dear; did he look sheepish?

MARIA. I am sure he has a susceptible heart, and

the ladies of his acquaintance must be very stupid not to——

CHARLOTTE. Hush! I hear some person coming.

*Enter* LETITIA

LETITIA. My dear Maria, I am happy to see you. Lud! what a pity it is that you have purchased your wedding clothes.

MARIA. I think so. [*Sighing.*

LETITIA. Why, my dear, there is the sweetest parcel of silks come over you ever saw! Nancy Brilliant has a full suit come; she sent over her measure, and it fits her to a hair; it is immensely dressy, and made for a court-hoop. I thought they said the large hoops were going out of fashion.

CHARLOTTE. Did you see the hat? Is it a fact that the deep laces round the border is still the fashion?

DIMPLE [*within*]. Upon my honour, Sir.

MARIA. Ha! Dimple's voice! My dear, I must take leave of you. There are some things necessary to be done at our house. Can't I go through the other room?

*Enter* DIMPLE *and* MANLY

DIMPLE. Ladies, your most obedient.

CHARLOTTE. Miss Van Rough, shall I present my brother Henry to you? Colonel Manly, Maria,— Miss Van Rough, brother.

MARIA. Her brother! [*Turns and sees* MANLY.] Oh! my heart! the very gentleman I have been prais, ing.

MANLY. The same amiable girl I saw this morning!

CHARLOTTE. Why, you look as if you were ac, quainted.

MANLY. I unintentionally intruded into this lady's presence this morning, for which she was so good as to promise me her forgiveness.

CHARLOTTE. Oh! ho! is that the case! Have these two penserosos been together? Were they Henry's eyes that looked so tenderly? [*Aside.*] And so you prom, ised to pardon him? and could you be so good, natured? have you really forgiven him? I beg you would do it for my sake [*whispering loud to* MARIA]. But, my dear, as you are in such haste, it would be cruel to detain you; I can show you the way through the other room.

MARIA. Spare me, my sprightly friend.

MANLY. The lady does not, I hope, intend to de, prive us of the pleasure of her company so soon.

CHARLOTTE. She has only a mantua, maker who waits for her at home. But, as I am to give my opin, ion of the dress, I think she cannot go yet. We were talking of the fashions when you came in, but I sup, pose the subject must be changed to something of more importance now. Mr. Dimple, will you favour us with an account of the public entertainments?

DIMPLE. Why, really, Miss Manly, you could not have asked me a question more *mal'apropos*. For my part, I must confess that, to a man who has travelled, there is nothing that is worthy the name of amuse ment to be found in this city.

CHARLOTTE. Except visiting the ladies.

DIMPLE. Pardon me, Madam; that is the avoca tion of a man of taste. But for amusement, I posi tively know of nothing that can be called so, unless you dignify with that title the hopping once a fort night to the sound of two or three squeaking fiddles, and the clattering of the old tavern windows, or sit ting to see the miserable mummers, whom you call actors, murder comedy and make a farce of tragedy.

MANLY. Do you never attend the theatre, Sir?

DIMPLE. I was tortured there once.

CHARLOTTE. Pray, Mr. Dimple, was it a tragedy or a comedy?

DIMPLE. Faith, Madam, I cannot tell; for I sat with my back to the stage all the time, admiring a much better actress than any there—a lady who played the fine woman to perfection; though, by the laugh of the horrid creatures round me, I suppose it was com edy. Yet, on second thoughts, it might be some hero in a tragedy, dying so comically as to set the whole house in an uproar. Colonel, I presume you have been in Europe?

MANLY. Indeed, Sir, I was never ten leagues from the continent.

DIMPLE. Believe me, Colonel, you have an immense pleasure to come; and when you shall have seen the brilliant exhibitions of Europe, you will learn to despise the amusements of this country as much as I do.

MANLY. Therefore I do not wish to see them; for I can never esteem that knowledge valuable which tends to give me a distaste for my native country.

DIMPLE. Well, Colonel, though you have not travelled, you have read.

MANLY. I have, a little; and by it have discovered that there is a laudable partiality which ignorant, untravelled men entertain for everything that belongs to their native country. I call it laudable; it injures no one; adds to their own happiness; and, when extended, becomes the noble principle of patriotism. Travelled gentlemen rise superior, in their own opinion, to this; but if the contempt which they contract for their country is the most valuable acquisition of their travels, I am far from thinking that their time and money are well spent.

MARIA. What noble sentiments!

CHARLOTTE. Let my brother set out where he will in the fields of conversation, he is sure to end his tour in the temple of gravity.

MANLY. Forgive me, my sister. I love my country; it has its foibles undoubtedly;—some foreigners will with pleasure remark them—but such remarks fall very ungracefully from the lips of her citizens.

DIMPLE. You are perfectly in the right, Colonel—America has her faults.

MANLY. Yes, Sir; and we, her children, should blush for them in private, and endeavour, as individuals, to reform them. But, if our country has its errors in common with other countries, I am proud to say America—I mean the United States—has displayed virtues and achievements which modern nations may admire, but of which they have seldom set us the example.

CHARLOTTE. But, brother, we must introduce you to some of our gay folks, and let you see the city, such as it is. Mr. Dimple is known to almost every family in town; he will doubtless take a pleasure in introducing you?

DIMPLE. I shall esteem every service I can render your brother an honour.

MANLY. I fear the business I am upon will take up all my time, and my family will be anxious to hear from me.

MARIA. His family! but what is it to me that he is married! [*Aside*.] Pray, how did you leave your lady, Sir?

CHARLOTTE. My brother is not married [*observing her anxiety*]; it is only an odd way he has of express' ing himself. Pray, brother, is this business, which you make your continual excuse, a secret?

MANLY. No, sister; I came hither to solicit the honourable Congress, that a number of my brave old soldiers may be put upon the pension'list, who were, at first, not judged to be so materially wounded as to need the public assistance. My sister says true [*to Ma' ria*]: I call my late soldiers my family. Those who were not in the field in the late glorious contest, and those who were, have their respective merits; but, I confess, my old brother'soldiers are dearer to me than the former description. Friendships made in adver' sity are lasting; our countrymen may forget us, but that is no reason why we should forget one another. But I must leave you; my time of engagement ap' proaches.

CHARLOTTE. Well, but, brother, if you will go, will you please to conduct my fair friend home? You live in the same street ———— I was to have gone with her myself—[*Aside.*] A lucky thought.

MARIA. I am obliged to your sister, Sir, and was just intending to go. [*Going.*

MANLY. I shall attend her with pleasure.

[*Exit with* MARIA, *followed by* DIMPLE *and* CHARLOTTE.

MARIA. Now, pray, don't betray me to your brother.

CHARLOTTE. [*Just as she sees him make a motion
to take his leave.*] One word with you, brother, if you
please.                                    [*Follows them out.*

[*Manent,* DIMPLE *and* LETITIA.

DIMPLE. You received the billet I sent you, I presume?

LETITIA. Hush!—Yes.

DIMPLE. When shall I pay my respects to you?

LETITIA. At eight I shall be unengaged.

*Reenter* CHARLOTTE

DIMPLE. Did my lovely angel receive my billet?
[*To* CHARLOTTE.]

CHARLOTTE. Yes.

DIMPLE. What hour shall I expect with impatience?

CHARLOTTE. At eight I shall be at home unengaged.

DIMPLE. Unfortunate! I have a horrid engagement of business at that hour. Can't you finish your
visit earlier and let six be the happy hour?

CHARLOTTE. You know your influence over me.
                                    [*Exeunt severally.*

## SCENE II

VAN ROUGH'S *House*

VAN ROUGH [*alone*]. It cannot possibly be true! The son of my old friend can't have acted so unadvisedly. Seventeen thousand pounds! in bills! Mr. Transfer must have been mistaken. He always appeared so prudent, and talked so well upon money matters, and even assured me that he intended to change his dress for a suit of clothes which would not cost so much, and look more substantial, as soon as he married. No, no, no! it can't be; it cannot be. But, however, I must look out sharp. I did not care what his principles or his actions were, so long as he minded the main chance. Seventeen thousand pounds! If he had lost it in trade, why the best men may have ill-luck; but to game it away, as Transfer says—why, at this rate, his whole estate may go in one night, and, what is ten times worse, mine into the bargain. No, no; Mary is right. Leave women to look out in these matters; for all they look as if they didn't know a journal from a ledger, when their interest is concerned they know what's what; they mind the main chance as well as the best of us. I wonder Mary did not tell me she knew of his spending his money so foolishly. Seventeen thousand pounds! Why, if my daughter was standing up to be married, I would forbid the banns, if I found it was to a man who did not mind the main chance.—Hush! I hear somebody coming. 'Tis Mary s voice; a man with her too! I shouldn't be surprised if this should be the other string to her bow. Aye, aye, let them alone; women under٫ stand the main chance.—Though, i' faith, I'll listen a little.                    [*Retires into a closet.*

MANLY *leading in* MARIA

MANLY. I hope you will excuse my speaking upon so important a subject so abruptly; but, the moment I entered your room, you struck me as the lady whom I had long loved in imagination, and never hoped to see.

MARIA. Indeed, Sir, I have been led to hear more upon this subject than I ought.

MANLY. Do you, then, disapprove my suit, Madam, or the abruptness of my introducing it? If the latter, my peculiar situation, being obliged to leave the city in a few days, will, I hope, be my excuse; if the for٫ mer, I will retire, for I am sure I would not give a moment's inquietude to her whom I could devote my life to please. I am not so indelicate as to seek your immediate approbation; permit me only to be near you, and by a thousand tender assiduities to en٫ deavour to excite a grateful return.

MARIA. I have a father, whom I would die to make happy; he will disapprove——

MANLY. Do you think me so ungenerous as to seek a place in your esteem without his consent? You must —you ever ought to consider that man as unworthy of you who seeks an interest in your heart contrary to a father's approbation. A young lady should reflect that the loss of a lover may be supplied, but nothing can compensate for the loss of a parent's affection. Yet, why do you suppose your father would disap⁄ prove? In our country, the affections are not sacrificed to riches or family aggrandizement: should you ap⁄ prove, my family is decent, and my rank honourable.

MARIA. You distress me, Sir.

MANLY. Then I will sincerely beg your excuse for obtruding so disagreeable a subject, and retire. [*Going.*

MARIA. Stay, Sir! your generosity and good opin⁄ ion of me deserve a return; but why must I declare what, for these few hours, I have scarce suffered my⁄ self to think?—I am ——

MANLY. What?

MARIA. Engaged, Sir; and, in a few days to be married to the gentleman you saw at your sister's.

MANLY. Engaged to be married! And I have been basely invading the rights of another? Why have you permitted this? Is this the return for the partiality I declared for you?

MARIA. You distress me, Sir. What would you have me say? you are too generous to wish the truth. Ought

I to say that I dared not suffer myself to think of my engagement, and that I am going to give my hand without my heart? Would you have me confess a partiality for you? If so, your triumph is compleat, and can be only more so when days of misery with the man I cannot love will make me think of him whom I could prefer.

MANLY [*after a pause*]. We are both unhappy; but it is your duty to obey your parent—mine to obey my honour. Let us, therefore, both follow the path of rectitude; and of this we may be assured, that if we are not happy, we shall, at least, deserve to be so. Adieu! I dare not trust myself longer with you.

[*Exeunt severally.*

### END OF THE FOURTH ACT

## ACT V. SCENE I

### Dimple's *Lodgings*

#### Jessamy *meeting* Jonathan

JESSAMY. Well, Mr. Jonathan, what success with the fair?

JONATHAN. Why, such a tarnal cross tike you never saw! You would have counted she had lived upon crab-apples and vinegar for a fortnight. But what the rattle makes you look so tarnation glum?

JESSAMY. I was thinking, Mr. Jonathan, what could be the reason of her carrying herself so coolly to you.

JONATHAN. Coolly, do you call it? Why, I vow, she was fire-hot angry: may be it was because I buss'd her.

JESSAMY. No, no, Mr. Jonathan; there must be some other cause; I never yet knew a lady angry at being kissed.

JONATHAN. Well, if it is not the young woman's bashfulness, I vow I can't conceive why she shouldn't like me.

JESSAMY. May be it is because you have not the Graces, Mr. Jonathan.

JONATHAN. Grace! Why, does the young woman expect I must be converted before I court her?

JESSAMY. I mean graces of person: for instance, my

lord tells us that we must cut off our nails even at top, in small segments of circles — though you won't understand that; in the next place, you must regulate your laugh.

JONATHAN. Maple-log seize it ! don t I laugh natural?

JESSAMY. That's the very fault, Mr. Jonathan. Besides, you absolutely misplace it. I was told by a friend of mine that you laughed outright at the play the other night, when you ought only to have tittered.

JONATHAN. Gor ! I — what does one go to see fun for if they can't laugh.

JESSAMY. You may laugh; but you must laugh by rule.

JONATHAN. Swamp it — laugh by rule ! Well, I should like that tarnally.

JESSAMY. Why, you know, Mr. Jonathan, that to dance, a lady to play with her fan, or a gentleman with his cane, and all other natural motions, are regulated by art. My master has composed an immensely pretty gamut, by which any lady or gentleman, with a few years' close application, may learn to laugh as gracefully as if they were born and bred to it.

JONATHAN. Mercy on my soul! A gamut for laughing — just like fa, la, sol?

JESSAMY. Yes. It comprises every possible display of jocularity, from an *affettuoso* smile to a *piano* titter,

or full chorus *fortissimo* ha, ha, ha! My master em-
ploys his leisure hours in marking out the plays, like a
cathedral chanting-book, that the ignorant may know
where to laugh; and that pit, box, and gallery may
keep time together, and not have a snigger in one part
of the house, a broad grin in the other, and a d——d
grum look in the third. How delightful to see the audience all smile together, then look on their books,
then twist their mouths into an agreeable simper, then
altogether shake the house with a general ha, ha, ha!
loud as a full chorus of Handel's at an Abbey com-
memoration.

JONATHAN. Ha, ha, ha! that's dang'd cute, I swear.

JESSAMY. The gentlemen, you see, will laugh the
tenor; the ladies will play the counter-tenor; the beaux
will squeak the treble; and our jolly friends in the gallery a thorough base, ho, ho, ho!

JONATHAN. Well, can't you let me see that gamut?

JESSAMY. Oh! yes, Mr. Jonathan; here it is [*Takes
out a book*.] Oh! no, this is only a titter with its variations. Ah, here it is. [*Takes out another*.] Now, you
must know, Mr. Jonathan, this is a piece written by
Ben Johnson, which I have set to my master's gamut.
The places where you must smile, look grave, or laugh
outright, are marked below the line. Now look over
me. "There was a certain man"—now you must
smile.

JONATHAN. Well, read it again; I warrant I'll mind my eye.

JESSAMY. "There was a certain man, who had a sad scolding wife," — now you must laugh.

JONATHAN. Tarnation! That's no laughing matter though.

JESSAMY. "And she lay sick a'dying"; — now you must titter.

JONATHAN. What, snigger when the good woman's a'dying! Gor, I——

JESSAMY. Yes, the notes say you must — "and she asked her husband leave to make a will," — now you must begin to look grave; "and her husband said"——

JONATHAN. Ay, what did her husband say? Some thing dang d cute, I reckon.

JESSAMY. "And her husband said, you have had your will all your life'time, and would you have it after you are dead, too?"

JONATHAN. Ho, ho, ho! There the old man was even with her; he was up to the notch — ha, ha, ha!

JESSAMY. But, Mr. Jonathan, you must not laugh so. Why you ought to have tittered *piano*, and you have laughed *fortissimo*. Look here; you see these marks, A, B, C, and so on; these are the references to the other part of the book. Let us turn to it, and you will see the directions how to manage the muscles. This [*turns over*] was note D you blundered at. — You

must purse the mouth into a smile, then titter, discov⸗
ering the lower part of the three front upper teeth.

JONATHAN. How? read it again.

JESSAMY. "There was a certain man"—very
well!—"who had a sad scolding wife,"—why don't
you laugh?

JONATHAN. Now, that scolding wife sticks in my
gizzard so pluckily that I can't laugh for the blood
and nowns of me. Let me look grave here, and I'll
laugh your belly full, where the old creature's a⸗dy⸗
ing.

JESSAMY. "And she asked her husband"—[*Bell
rings.*] My master's bell! he's returned, I fear.—Here,
Mr. Jonathan, take this gamut; and I make no doubt
but with a few years' close application, you may be
able to smile gracefully. [*Exeunt severally.*

## SCENE II

### CHARLOTTE'S *Apartment*

#### *Enter* MANLY

MANLY. What, no one at home? How unfortu⸗
nate to meet the only lady my heart was ever moved
by, to find her engaged to another, and confessing her
partiality for me! Yet engaged to a man who, by her
intimation, and his libertine conversation with me, I
fear, does not merit her. Aye! there's the sting; for,

were I assured that Maria was happy, my heart is not so selfish but that it would dilate in knowing it, even though it were with another. But to know she is unhappy!—I must drive these thoughts from me. Charlotte has some books; and this is what I believe she calls her little library. [*Enters a closet.*

*Enter* DIMPLE *leading* LETITIA

LETITIA. And will you pretend to say now, Mr. Dimple, that you propose to break with Maria? Are not the banns published? Are not the clothes purchased? Are not the friends invited? In short, is it not a done affair?

DIMPLE. Believe me, my dear Letitia, I would not marry her.

LETITIA. Why have you not broke with her before this, as you all along deluded me by saying you would?

DIMPLE. Because I was in hopes she would, ere this, have broke with me.

LETITIA. You could not expect it.

DIMPLE. Nay, but be calm a moment; 'twas from my regard to you that I did not discard her.

LETITIA. Regard to me!

DIMPLE. Yes; I have done everything in my power to break with her, but the foolish girl is so fond of me that nothing can accomplish it. Besides, how can

I offer her my hand when my heart is indissolubly engaged to you?

LETITIA. There may be reason in this; but why so
attentive to Miss Manly?

DIMPLE. Attentive to Miss Manly! For heaven s
sake, if you have no better opinion of my constancy,
pay not so ill a compliment to my taste.

LETITIA. Did I not see you whisper her to-day?

DIMPLE. Possibly I might — but something of so
very trifling a nature that I have already forgot what
it was.

LETITIA. I believe she has not forgot it.

DIMPLE. My dear creature, how can you for a moment suppose I should have any serious thoughts
of that trifling, gay, flighty coquette, that disagreeable ——

*Enter* CHARLOTTE

My dear Miss Manly, I rejoice to see you; there
is a charm in your conversation that always marks
your entrance into company as fortunate.

LETITIA. Where have you been, my dear?

CHARLOTTE. Why, I have been about to twenty
shops, turning over pretty things, and so have left
twenty visits unpaid. I wish you would step into
the carriage and whisk round, make my apology,
and leave my cards where our friends are not at

home; that, you know, will serve as a visit. Come, do go.

LETITIA. So anxious to get me out! but I'll watch you. [*Aside.*] Oh! yes, I'll go; I want a little exer‚ cise. Positively [DIMPLE *offering to accompany her*], Mr. Dimple, you shall not go; why, half my visits are cake and candle visits; it won't do, you know, for you to go.

> [*Exit, but returns to the door in the back scene and listens.*

DIMPLE. This attachment of your brother to Maria is fortunate.

CHARLOTTE. How did you come to the knowledge of it?

DIMPLE. I read it in their eyes.

CHARLOTTE. And I had it from her mouth. It would have amused you to have seen her! She, that thought it so great an impropriety to praise a gentle‚ man that she could not bring out one word in your favour, found a redundancy to praise him.

DIMPLE. I have done everything in my power to assist his passion there: your delicacy, my dearest girl, would be shocked at half the instances of neg‚ lect and misbehaviour.

CHARLOTTE. I don't know how I should bear neg‚ lect; but Mr. Dimple must misbehave himself in‚ deed, to forfeit my good opinion.

DIMPLE. Your good opinion, my angel, is the pride and pleasure of my heart; and if the most respectful tenderness for you, and an utter indifference for all your sex besides, can make me worthy of your esteem, I shall richly merit it.

CHARLOTTE. All my sex besides, Mr. Dimple! — you forgot your tete⁄a⁄tete with Letitia.

DIMPLE. How can you, my lovely angel, cast a thought on that insipid, wry⁄mouthed, ugly creature!

CHARLOTTE. But her fortune may have charms.

DIMPLE. Not to a heart like mine. The man, who has been blessed with the good opinion of my Char⁄lotte, must despise the allurements of fortune.

CHARLOTTE. I am satisfied.

DIMPLE. Let us think no more on the odious sub⁄ject, but devote the present hour to happiness.

CHARLOTTE. Can I be happy, when I see the man I prefer going to be married to another?

DIMPLE. Have I not already satisfied my charming angel, that I can never think of marrying the puling Maria? But, even if it were so, could that be any bar to our happiness? for, as the poet sings,

> " Love, free as air, at sight of human ties,
>     Spreads his light wings, and in a moment flies."

Come, then, my charming angel! why delay our bliss? The present moment is ours; the next is in the hand of fate. [*Kissing her.*

CHARLOTTE. Begone, Sir! By your delusions you had almost lulled my honour asleep.

DIMPLE. Let me lull the demon to sleep again with kisses. [*He struggles with her; she screams.*

*Enter* MANLY

MANLY. Turn, villain! and defend yourself.——
[*Draws.*

VAN ROUGH *enters and beats down their swords*

VAN ROUGH. Is the devil in you? are you going to murder one another? [*Holding* DIMPLE.

DIMPLE. Hold him, hold him,— I can command my passion.

*Enter* JONATHAN

JONATHAN. What the rattle ails you? Is the old one in you? Let the colonel alone, can t you? I feel chock full of fight, — do you want to kill the colonel?——

MANLY. Be still, Jonathan; the gentleman does not want to hurt me.

JONATHAN. Gor! I—I wish he did; I'd shew him Yankee boys play, pretty quick. — Don't you see you have frightened the young woman into the *hystrikes?*

VAN ROUGH. Pray, some of you explain this; what has been the occasion of all this racket?

MANLY. That gentleman can explain it to you; it

will be a very diverting story for an intended father-in-law to hear.

VAN ROUGH. How was this matter, Mr. Van Dumpling?

DIMPLE. Sir,—upon my honour,—all I know is, that I was talking to this young lady, and this gentleman broke in on us in a very extraordinary manner.

VAN ROUGH. Why, all this is nothing to the purpose; can you explain it, Miss?     [*To* CHARLOTTE.

*Enter* LETITIA *through the back scene*

LETITIA. I can explain it to that gentleman's confusion. Though long betrothed to your daughter [*to* VAN ROUGH], yet, allured by my fortune, it seems (with shame do I speak it) he has privately paid his addresses to me. I was drawn in to listen to him by his assuring me that the match was made by his father without his consent, and that he proposed to break with Maria, whether he married me or not. But, whatever were his intentions respecting your daughter, Sir, even to me he was false; for he has repeated the same story, with some cruel reflections upon my person, to Miss Manly.

JONATHAN. What a tarnal curse!

LETITIA. Nor is this all, Miss Manly. When he was with me this very morning, he made the same ungenerous reflections upon the weakness of your mind as he has so recently done upon the defects of my person.

JONATHAN. What a tarnal curse and damn, too.

DIMPLE. Ha! since I have lost Letitia, I believe I had as good make it up with Maria. Mr. Van Rough, at present I cannot enter into particulars; but, I believe, I can explain everything to your satisfaction in private.

VAN ROUGH. There is another matter, Mr. Van Dumpling, which I would have you explain. Pray, Sir, have Messrs. Van Cash & Co. presented you those bills for acceptance?

DIMPLE. The deuce! Has he heard of those bills! Nay, then, all's up with Maria, too; but an affair of this sort can never prejudice me among the ladies; they will rather long to know what the dear creature possesses to make him so agreeable. [*Aside*.] Sir, you'll hear from me.                    [*To* MANLY.

MANLY. And you from me, Sir ——

DIMPLE. Sir, you wear a sword ——

MANLY. Yes, Sir. This sword was presented to me by that brave Gallic hero, the Marquis De la Fayette. I have drawn it in the service of my country, and in private life, on the only occasion where a man is justified in drawing his sword, in defence of a lady's honour. I have fought too many battles in the service of my country to dread the imputation of cowardice.

Death from a man of honour would be a glory you do not merit; you shall live to bear the insult of man and the contempt of that sex whose general smiles afforded you all your happiness.

DIMPLE. You won t meet me, Sir? Then I'll post you for a coward.

MANLY. I'll venture that, Sir. The reputation of my life does not depend upon the breath of a Mr. Dimple. I would have you to know, however, Sir, that I have a cane to chastise the insolence of a scoun⁄drel, and a sword and the good laws of my country to protect me from the attempts of an assassin——

DIMPLE. Mighty well! Very fine, indeed! Ladies and gentlemen, I take my leave; and you will please to observe in the case of my deportment the contrast between a gentleman who has read Chesterfield and received the polish of Europe and an unpolished, un⁄travelled American.                    [*Exit.*

*Enter* MARIA

MARIA. Is he indeed gone?——

LETITIA. I hope, never to return.

VAN ROUGH. I am glad I heard of those bills; though it's plaguy unlucky; I hoped to see Mary mar⁄ried before I died.

MANLY. Will you permit a gentleman, Sir, to offer himself as a suitor to your daughter? Though a stran⁄

ger to you, he is not altogether so to her, or unknown in this city. You may find a son-in-law of more fortune, but you can never meet with one who is richer in love for her, or respect for you.

VAN ROUGH. Why, Mary, you have not let this gentleman make love to you without my leave?

MANLY. I did not say, Sir ——

MARIA. Say, Sir!——I—the gentleman, to be sure, met me accidentally.

VAN ROUGH. Ha, ha, ha! Mark me, Mary; young folks think old folks to be fools; but old folks know young folks to be fools. Why, I knew all about this affair. This was only a cunning way I had to bring it about. Hark ye! I was in the closet when you and he were at our house. [*Turns to the company.*] I heard that little baggage say she loved her old father, and would die to make him happy! Oh! how I loved the little baggage! And you talked very prudently, young man. I have inquired into your character, and find you to be a man of punctuality and mind the main chance. And so, as you love Mary and Mary loves you, you shall have my consent immediately to be married. I'll settle my fortune on you, and go and live with you the remainder of my life.

MANLY. Sir, I hope ——

VAN ROUGH. Come, come, no fine speeches; mind the main chance, young man, and you and I shall always agree.

LETITIA. I sincerely wish you joy [*advancing to* MARIA]; and hope your pardon for my conduct.

MARIA. I thank you for your congratulations, and hope we shall at once forget the wretch who has given us so much disquiet, and the trouble that he has occasioned.

CHARLOTTE. And I, my dear Maria, — how shall I look up to you for forgiveness? I, who, in the practice of the meanest arts, have violated the most sacred rights of friendship? I never can forgive myself, or hope charity from the world; but, I confess, I have much to hope from such a brother; and I am happy that I may soon say, such a sister.

MARIA. My dear, you distress me; you have all my love.

MANLY. And mine.

CHARLOTTE. If repentance can entitle me to forgiveness, I have already much merit; for I despise the littleness of my past conduct. I now find that the heart of any worthy man cannot be gained by invidious attacks upon the rights and characters of others; — by countenancing the addresses of a thousand; — or that the finest assemblage of features, the greatest taste in dress, the genteelest address, or the most brilliant wit, cannot eventually secure a coquette from contempt and ridicule.

MANLY. And I have learned that probity, virtue,

honour, though they should not have received the polish of Europe, will secure to an honest American the good graces of his fair countrywomen, and I hope, the applause of THE PUBLIC.

## THE END

# REVIVALS OF "THE CONTRAST"

By pupils of the American Academy of Dramatic Arts, New York, 1894.[1]

By townsmen, in Brattleboro, Vermont, at the Brattleboro Pageant, June 6, 7, and 8, 1912. Beautifully and correctly performed, well acted, accorded an enthusiastic reception.

By the Play and Players of Philadelphia, of the Drama League of America, in cooperation with the University of Pennsylvania, January 16 and 18, 1917. Full and appreciative audiences found the old comedy interesting. The newspaper comments were favorable as to the permanency of value in the comedy.

By the American Drama Committee of the Drama League of America, New York Centre, January 22 and 23, 1917, the conversation between Jonathan and Jenny.

By the Drama League of Boston, April 7, 1917. Reproduced as nearly as possible, designs, costumes, and staging of original period. The audience responded, as of yore,[2] " with applause," and the newspapers published long critical reviews, finding much vitality in the play — as well as many demerits.

[1] *Springfield Republican*, March 18, 1894.
[2] From criticisms of performances of *The Contrast: Daily Advertiser*, New York, April 18, 1787 : " . . . the unceasing plaudits of the audience "; *The Maryland Journal and Baltimore Advertiser*, November 16, 1787 : " . . . with reiterated bursts of applause. "

# LIST OF WORKS OF ROYALL TYLER

THE CONTRAST. A Comedy. First acted, *April* 16, 1787. Published by Thomas Wignell, Philadelphia, 1790. Reprinted by Dunlap Society, New York, 1887.

MAY DAY IN TOWN ; or, NEW YORK IN AN UPROAR. New York, *May* 19, 1787.

THE ORIGIN OF EVIL. An Elegy. 1792. ⎱

ODE TO NIGHT. 1792. ⎰

In original manuscript, owned by Helen Tyler Brown, Brattleboro, Vermont.

THE DOCTOR IN SPITE OF HIMSELF. A Comedy. *Date uncertain.*

THE FARM HOUSE ; or, THE FEMALE DUELLISTS. A Farce. Boston, 1796.

THE GEORGIA SPEC ; or, LAND IN THE MOON. A Comedy, ridiculing speculations in wild Yazoo lands. Boston and New York, 1797–1798.

Note in *Columbian Centinel*, Boston, October 28, 1797:

"The Georgia Spec, or Land in the Moon, a Comedy in three acts, is said by judges who have read it in manuscript, to be the best production that has flowed from the ingenious pen of R. Tyler, Esq. It contains a rich diversity of national character and native humour, scarcely to be found in any other drama in the language. In a play, founded on incidents at home, the author deserves great credit for the circumspect candour, with which he has avoided every species of personality.

"The characters are all taken from general life, without any appropriate reference whatever. Replete with incident, enlivened by wit, and amply fraught with harmless mirth, the Comedy is entitled to the applause of all without wounding the feelings of any."

THE ALGERINE CAPTIVE ; or, THE LIFE AND ADVENTURES OF DOCTOR UPDIKE UNDERHILL : SIX YEARS A PRISONER AMONG THE

ALGERINES. 2 Vols. Walpole, New Hampshire, Davis Carlisle, 1797. 2 Vols. in 1. Hartford, Connecticut, Peter B. Gleason Co., 1816. 2 Vols. London, England, G. and J. Robinson, Paternoster Row, 1802.

This was one of the first American works to be republished in England, and completely deceived the public, being considered a genuine narrative.

MORAL TALES FOR AMERICAN YOUTH. J. Nancrede, Boston, 1800.

REPORTS OF CASES IN THE SUPREME COURT OF VERMONT. 2 Vols. 1809–10.

THE YANKEY IN LONDON, being the First Part of a Series of Letters Written by an American Youth, during nine Months Residence in the city of London; Addressed to his Friends in and near Boston, Massachusetts. Volume 1. New York, 1809.

THE SHOP OF MESSRS. COLON AND SPONDEE. (In collaboration with Joseph Dennie.) Political squibs and comments on news of the day, satirizing fashionable follies and manners. *The Farmer's Weekly Museum*, Walpole, New Hampshire, 1794–99. Royall Tyler was "Spondee."

This was a popular paper. Its circulation was extensive, and it was in Washington's library at Mount Vernon.

ORATION ON THE DEATH OF WASHINGTON. 1800. (Manuscript copy extant.)

THE MANTLE OF WASHINGTON. An Address delivered on the Anniversary of his Birthday. 1800. (Manuscript copy extant.)

ODE FOR THE FOURTH OF JULY. 1799.

See Duyckinck's *Cyclopedia of American Literature*, Vol. 1. 1855.

*The Spirit of The Farmer's Museum and Lay Preacher's Gazette*, published by David Carlisle, Walpole, New Hampshire, 1801. A collection of verse and prose taken from the files of *The Farmer's Weekly Museum*. Contained many specimens of Royall Tyler's verse and prose; also Joseph Dennie's and others'.

Occasional contributions in Joseph Dennie's periodical, *The Portfolio*, under the titles of AN AUTHOR'S EVENINGS and ORIGINAL POETRY. Philadelphia, 1801–12.

Trash. A series of articles in J. T. Buckingham's *Polyanthos*. Boston, 1806.

Love and Liberty and The Chestnut Tree have been called his best poems. *Dates uncertain.*

For "Love and Liberty" see Duyckinck's *Cyclopedia of American Literature*, Vol. 1. 1855. For "The Bookworm," taken from the manuscript copy of "The Chestnut Tree," see *Library of American Literature*, Stedman and Hutchinson.

Royall Tyler contributed other verse and prose in many contemporary periodicals such as *The Federal Orrery*, *Boston Columbian Centinel*, *Boston Eagle* or *Dartmouth Centinel*, *New England Galaxy*, and Vermont newspapers. A complete list has not been attempted.

During his long and wasting illness he wrote constantly, leaving unpublished three sacred dramas, "The Origin of the Feast of Purim, or The Destinies of Haman and Mordecai," "Joseph and His Brethren," and "The Judgment of Solomon"; a comedy, "Tantalization, or The Governor of a Day"; poems, "Fables for Children" and "The Bay Boy, A Tale" (unfinished). He also left manuscript notes of a Comic Grammar and an Opera and outlines of projected works.

TWO HUNDRED AND SEVENTY-FIVE COPIES OF THIS BOOK, OF
WHICH TWO HUNDRED AND FIFTY ARE FOR SALE, WERE
PRINTED AT THE RIVERSIDE PRESS IN CAMBRIDGE, MASSA-
CHUSETTS.

THIS IS NUMBER..........

The Riverside Press

CAMBRIDGE . MASSACHUSETTS

U . S . A

0 015 861 862 A

Made in the USA
Middletown, DE
25 January 2019